Fear-fed adrenaline surged through her

Then as suddenly as it started, the attack was over. He released her and stepped back, holding the gun.

"Sorry," RJ told her. "My house, my rules."

He opened the cylinder and dropped the shells into the palm of his hand. Tossing them to her, he held her gaze.

"You keep the bullets. I'll keep the gun."

She was trembling all over, from shock and fear.

"Feel free to leave if you want, but if you go out to your car, you won't be coming back inside tonight."

Teri believed him. She knew he had no reason to trust her or to know if she had another weapon in the car.

"For what it's worth, Teri, if I'd wanted to attack you, I'd have done so. I prefer a willing partner."

RETURN TO STONY RIDGE

DANI SINCLAIR

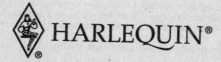

HARLEQUIN®

TORONTO • NEW YORK • LONDON
AMSTERDAM • PARIS • SYDNEY • HAMBURG
STOCKHOLM • ATHENS • TOKYO • MILAN • MADRID
PRAGUE • WARSAW • BUDAPEST • AUCKLAND

For women of courage everywhere.
Special thanks to Judy Fitzpatrick, Natashya Wilson
and my own hero, Roger.
I couldn't have done this without you guys.
And of course, for Chip and Dan and Barb as always.

ISBN 0-373-22870-8

RETURN TO STONY RIDGE

Copyright © 2005 by Patricia A. Gagne

ABOUT THE AUTHOR

An avid reader, Dani Sinclair didn't discover romance novels until her mother lent her one when she'd come for a visit. Dani's been hooked on the genre ever since. But she didn't take up writing seriously until her two sons were grown. With the premiere of *Mystery Baby* for Harlequin Intrigue in 1996, Dani's kept her computer busy ever since. Her third novel, *Better Watch Out,* was a RITA® Award finalist in 1998. Dani lives outside Washington, D.C., a place she's found to be a great source for both intrigue and humor!

You can write to her in care of the Harlequin Reader Service.

Books by Dani Sinclair

HARLEQUIN INTRIGUE

Don't miss any of our special offers. Write to us at the following address for information on our newest releases.

Harlequin Reader Service
U.S.: 3010 Walden Ave., P.O. Box 1325, Buffalo, NY 14269
Canadian: P.O. Box 609, Fort Erie, Ont. L2A 5X3

CAST OF CHARACTERS

Teri Johnson—This intriguing P.I. has a whopping secret.

RJ Monroe—Helping an old friend may have put this contractor in a killer's sights.

Olivia Barnesly—Teri's mysterious client has never met the woman she hired Teri to find.

Valerie Boyington—This desperate mother went missing in the dead of night.

Corey Boyington—Valerie's son is safe—and safely hidden.

Lester Boyington—The businessman seems genuinely worried about his missing wife and son.

Wyatt Crossley—The police chief has his hands full.

Will Leftcowitz—He wasn't always a groundskeeper.

Mrs. Norwhich—The cook may be lacking in personality, but she makes a mean sandwich.

George and Emily Walken—The kind older couple have taken in foster children for most of their married lives.

Kathy Walsh—The housekeeper can relate to the women at Heartskeep.

Ian, Nola and Boone—The kids swear there's someone—or some*thing*—moving around Heartskeep after dark.

Lucky—RJ's dog has lived up to his name more than once.

Prologue

Rain lashed the car. It was all he could do to hold it steady as the storm swirled around them. He could barely see the narrow, twisting road despite the frequent tongues of lightning in the night sky. Next to him, his wife slumped still and silent, her head flopping against the side window. In the backseat, the baby cried. The woman beside the baby stirred and moaned softly.

Finally, his straining headlights picked up the gleam of metal on the side of the road. Pulling up beside the parked vehicle, he stopped. In seconds, he was drenched as he transferred the crying child from the small car to the larger SUV.

Returning to the car, he hauled his sister-in-law's half-conscious form from the backseat and placed her behind the steering column of the small car. Despite her bruised face, she managed to open one eye and look at him accusingly.

"You should have minded your own business," he told her. He swung, enjoying the power as his fist smashed into her face once more and he felt her cheek-bone shatter. Her head pitched forward, hitting the steering wheel. Even though there was no one around to hear, he was glad she missed the horn. He positioned her body carefully, placing her foot on the gas pedal and using her heavy purse to hold it there. Lowering both side windows, he moved her unresisting hands to the wheel and glanced toward his wife. She hadn't moved, though he had jostled her getting her sister into position. Her head now slumped forward, away from the window. It was possible she was already dead. He didn't bother to check.

The roadway slanted steeply toward the narrow bridge over Leary Creek. Water lapped at the road, inching its way up the black surface in his direction. The top of the guardrail was the only visible indication of where the bridge stood. The creek was a swollen, raging river after two days of continuous heavy rain, and the angry water continued to rise with impossible speed, cascading across the bridge with a terrible roar.

Aiming the car, he put it in gear and quickly leaped back out of the way. The car lurched forward, gathering speed as it rolled toward the rising water.

Lightning and thunder crashed overhead. He watched the car plunge into the water where it was caught in the fierce current. The small vehicle instantly began drifting in the direction of the water's flow—over the bridge. Impatiently, he waited as it hung on the guardrail until a wave of debris-filled water washed against it with stunning force. The car was lifted and sent tumbling along with the swiftly flowing current until the open windows invited the waves inside. The car sank from view a moment later.

He tossed the roiling water a jaunty salute. "Goodbye, wife."

Then he hurried back to his son and the dry warmth of the waiting SUV.

Chapter One

The darkness beyond the rain-streaked window was as tempting as it was scary. Ten-year-old Ian Sutter peered through the pane of glass at the blurry line of trees that formed a forbidding barrier stopping the expansive lawn in its tracks. The tree's ghostly limbs swayed ominously as a gust of wind sped by.

Ian shivered. Had he really seen something move in their stark depths? He surveyed the dark bedroom. He wanted to climb back into bed and curl up beneath the covers, but he couldn't do that. He was late. It was past time to start his patrol. His mother slept soundly in the big bed across from him. It wouldn't do to wake her.

He felt the familiar coil of helplessness when he thought about his mom. Ian hated that he was only ten. He wanted to be older, bigger, stronger. Strong enough to keep anyone from ever hurting her again.

Ian slid out of bed. He patrolled the scary old house every night to be sure no one had found a way inside after the adults had gone to bed. His mother believed they were safe behind the gates and locked doors of

Heartskeep, but Ian didn't believe it for a minute. They'd never be safe if *he* found out where they were.

Patrolling was important. Flashlight in hand, Ian slipped out the door and started down the narrow back staircase. Mrs. Norwhich, the cook, always left a night-light on in the huge kitchen, but tonight there was no light. The room was a vast black shadow despite the bank of windows along the rear wall.

Ian shivered. He wasn't afraid of the dark. He was cold, that was all. His flashlight beam swept the empty room, allowing shadows to dance about the walls. He clicked the beam off to conserve his batteries and crossed to check that the alarm system was softly glowing red. It was. And the door was bolted, as it should have been. By touch he could also tell that each window was locked.

About to turn away, he froze. Something had moved outside. Heart pounding, he waited, his eyes straining to see across the grass to the opening where the maze led toward the fountain. At first, nothing happened, but he knew he hadn't imagined the motion. An indistinct figure suddenly appeared in the maze opening. It stood as still as death, barely visible as it gazed up at the house. Ian drew back hastily. The figure vanished. He was almost certain it had been the blond ghost.

He waited for several long minutes, but nothing else moved.

A man or a ghost?

Ian panted as excitement warred with fear. He wanted it to be the ghost. He was far less afraid of ghosts. Unless…would the ghost be angry he'd been spying? Would it come for him if it was?

The ghost wouldn't hurt him. Ghosts couldn't hurt people.

Could they?

For a moment, he wondered if he should tell someone what he'd seen. Not his mother. He'd just upset her, and she wouldn't believe him, anyhow. She hadn't before when he'd tried to tell her about the man who'd disappeared in the corner of the dining room. She'd told him she didn't believe in ghosts. Then she'd hugged him with her good arm and started to cry. He didn't like to make his mother cry. It made him feel all sick inside.

Mrs. Walsh would listen. She always listened. But even she would think he'd been dreaming. Ian continued to stare out toward the maze. Leaves kicked about by the slight breeze rustled across the grass. Nothing else moved.

He fingered his flashlight nervously. He was pretty sure ghosts couldn't hurt people. Better to finish his rounds and go back upstairs. There was nothing anyone could do about a ghost. But he'd hurry just in case it came inside again.

A SOFT CLOUD OF MIST drifted above the eerie trees and began to settle like a fine white shroud, blurring the dark ribbon of road stretching before her. Her headlights cut such a dim swath through the darkness they were all but useless. White-knuckled, Teri Johnson gripped the steering wheel as the trees swayed overhead. She forced tired eyes to stare through the windshield, pretty sure she was lost again.

Her instinctive dislike of the mysterious R.J. Monroe escalated another notch. If not for his interference she could have rescued Valerie and Corey this morning. She'd been so close!

Teri blinked wearily. Her need for sleep was growing critical. The few winks she'd snatched on the front seat of her car while waiting for the fog to dissipate this morning hadn't been nearly enough. Every time she thought about how close she'd come to being caught inside the old farmhouse, adrenaline jazzed her all over again.

She'd been driving for eight to ten hours now, thanks to that blasted detour, and if she didn't find the turnoff leading to Monroe's place in another few minutes she was going to…

What? Turn around and go back? Not an option.

Pull over and have a good cry? Certainly appealing, but a waste of time.

Where was the blasted turnoff? The man at the gas station hadn't implied it was this far out. But what had he said? She couldn't remember and the mist was turning to rain, making visibility a joke.

She heard the raspy sound of her breathing in the quiet of the car as her tension increased. She could no longer see the asphalt well enough to spot any standing water before she drove into it. She had to turn back.

Then she spotted a road to her left unmarked by lights. Only a dim reflection off the street sign told her she'd found her turn. In her relief and haste, she didn't see the water until it was splashing against the car wheels, bringing her heart into her throat.

Teri drew a ragged breath of relief as she cleared the water. Her hands were slick and they trembled. What had she been thinking? She should have waited for morning. She was too tired for a confrontation tonight.

"Heck of a time to come to that decision."

And she was talking to herself again. Great.

This was a bad idea. She really should turn around, find a motel for the night and come back first thing in the morning. But up ahead was a badly listing mailbox.

Without it, Teri would have driven past without spotting the narrow driveway.

She braked. There was no name on the mailbox, but this had to be the place. The attendant had said the house was well off the main road, but this entrance couldn't have been better hidden if it had been planned that way.

Maybe it had been.

Or maybe she was in the wrong place completely. Would a building contractor have a gravel driveway this deeply rutted and in such serious need of repair? Towering trees waved and bent overhead. The wind was doing its best to shake the leaves from their branches. Beginning to yellow for the season, they flattened across her windshield, clinging to the glass and defying the wipers that threatened to rip them aside.

And as the small coupe jounced and splashed its way over the deep ruts, her misgivings turned to certainty. Driving up to a stranger's front door at this hour of the night was a stupid thing to do. Teri knew nothing about R.J. Monroe except that he'd come between her and her goal. Maybe she should think through her approach instead of simply barging up there and challenging the man. What if he wasn't alone?

What if he *was?*

Spotting a small break in the trees lining the right side of the driveway, Teri slipped the car into the grassy clearing and switched off the headlights. The house, ablaze with lights, loomed ahead. She stared at the lovely old structure, hungry for repairs to the sagging front porch and the chipped, damaged gingerbread finish. The clapboards badly needed paint, while the weedy, overgrown front yard cried out for pruning and decent landscaping.

If Monroe was a general contractor, would his place really look like this? Talk about bad advertising. But maybe he'd just bought the house and was planning to restore it. There was a stately grandeur about the structure that had appeal despite its condition.

Thunder boomed overhead, drawing her out of her strange reverie. The rain had become a storm sweeping in undetected. Although every minute counted, common sense told her to head back to civilization until morning.

But she was so *close.*

And so was the storm bringing more rain. Water already pooled at the bottom of this street. More rain meant deeper water.

Putting the car in reverse, Teri backed under the trees in an effort to get the car turned around. The rear wheels began to sink.

"No!"

Bogged in mud, the tires spun uselessly. Sweating, she tried to calm, rocking the car forward and back. She didn't have to get out and look to know she had made the situation worse. She was good and stuck unless she got some traction under those rear wheels.

Cursing, she put the car in Park and turned off the engine, mentally running through the items she had with her. She had nothing that would work. There was no help for it. She was going to have to go to the house now, if only to get some assistance.

It would be okay. She'd scope out Monroe while pretending to be a lost motorist who'd made a wrong turn. Removing her gun from her purse, Teri stuffed her keys in her pocket, pulled the hood of her jacket up around her head and stepped outside.

Immediately, wind whipped the hood down and

back and sent her hair flying about her exposed face. Rain pummeled her skin. Yanking the hood back into place, she closed the car door, gave a furious glare at the half-buried rear wheel and hurried toward the brightly lit windows. Water soaked her tennis shoes and jeans in seconds.

Caution made her stop shy of the covered front porch on a rise of ground that allowed her to see inside the house clearly. The downstairs windows were bare of drapes. A string of bright floodlights illuminated the main rooms where a dusty, masculine figure bent over a makeshift worktable in the opening between the living and dining rooms.

As he straightened, she saw he was tall and lean and extremely well-muscled. His torso was bare to the waist. A pair of ragged, hacked-off jeans hardly decent enough to be called shorts covered a minimum of skin. They displayed distressingly muscular thighs and long, fit legs covered in a fine white dust like the rest of him. Thick white socks, heavy work boots, and a pair of goggles completed his attire. He definitely looked like a contractor.

It was something of a relief to see that. Obviously he had purchased the place to fix it up. Dust swirled in the air, stirred by the two giant oscillating fans he had running. They didn't stem the sweat that sheened off the hard planes of his chest under the intensely bright lights. All the windows were closed against the storm.

Teri watched as he tugged off the goggles and rolled those firm shoulders to stretch bunched muscles. Sweat trickled down one high cheekbone, leaving a visible trail in the dust that coated his tanned face around the line left by the goggles. He wiped at it absently with the back of his arm, leaving streaks of dirt behind.

He looked tired and brooding and magnificent. She tamped down that last thought instantly as he ran long fingers through lightly curling dark hair—almost, but not quite, in need of a trim—that clung to the back of his neck.

Teri hadn't expected him to be so big—or so strong—or so angry-looking. That last gave her pause, but at the same time there was something almost compelling about him. Mesmerized, she watched him lift a trimmed panel of drywall with an ease belied by the bunch and pull of muscles that strained across his back. For a lean man, he was deliciously well-developed. He worked the panel into place against the bared furring with deft experience. Hefting a hammer, he drove the nails in with precise hard, almost rhythmic blows that sent her blood hammering as well.

There was quiet symmetry in the way he moved, completely focused on his task. As he turned to pick up a tape measure, she had an unrestricted view of his face. The symmetry carried to his features as well. He was unsettlingly handsome, and he appeared to be completely alone until a large black animal lifted its head from its curled position on the floor.

Teri froze. The dog gathered itself slowly and stood. It shook itself and stopped. It seemed to look straight at her.

She told herself he couldn't possibly see her, but she didn't move. For the first time in several minutes, she became aware of her surroundings. The storm was growing in intensity. She couldn't have been wetter if she'd gone swimming fully clothed. And she was cold. So cold her teeth were starting to chatter.

Coming here tonight had been stupid. She didn't know what she'd expected, but this dark brooding man and his big dog weren't it. He continued working with an economy of movement that she might have appreciated under other circumstances, but she'd swear the large dog's gaze remained focused on her.

Better to spend another night in her car under the trees than knock on that door. There was nothing the least bit welcoming in the man's dark scowl or the dog's intent stare.

Lightning speared the sky. Teri turned and ran, driven by the echo of thunder in her ears.

FRUSTRATION DROVE every blow of the hammer. Guilt and anger ate at R.J. in equal parts. He'd promised Valerie she'd be safe at Heartskeep. Yet she'd gone missing all the same. Either she'd played him for a fool or he should have done more to keep her safe.

He hoped it was the former. He wasn't sure he could live with the guilt if the person responsible for her battered condition had managed to get to her despite all the safeguards they had in place at Heartskeep.

He hadn't seen Valerie since her brother's funeral several years ago. Then she'd been a teenager, inconsolable over the death of the big brother who'd died so senselessly in a military training exercise. R.J. had wanted to cry as well as they lowered his best friend into the ground. And even though he'd lost touch with the family after they moved away a few months later, he'd never forget the debt he owed Eric and his family.

When the rest of Stony Ridge had labeled R.J. a troublemaker and worse, Eric's family had welcomed him into their home, treating him as they did all Eric's friends, making him feel at ease the same way his foster parents had done.

Lightning flared so close that a thunderclap rattled the windows. Without warning, the house plunged into cavernous black and abrupt silence, save for the howling of the wind and the battering rain.

R.J. tore his thoughts from the past and swore. "Great. Just great."

Lucky suddenly flew to the front door. The low, deep growl of warning that issued from his throat captured R.J.'s full attention.

"It's just a storm, fella."

Lucky clawed at the door intently, demanding it open.

"What's wrong, boy?"

Not a deer or squirrel. Not in this storm. And as the skies lit once more, he glimpsed a human figure running down the drive.

Valerie?

The surge of hope had him twisting the doorknob before his brain could assimilate how unlikely that was. She didn't know where he lived.

Lucky shouldered the door aside before he could grab the dog's collar and bounded out into the storm.

"Lucky! Get back here!"

He might as well have ordered the wind. Lucky plunged down the steps as if all hell wasn't breaking loose around him. R.J. cursed and went after him. He was pretty sure Lucky wouldn't hurt anyone, but he'd never heard the big dog growl like that before.

In a wicked display of light and noise, a large tree limb crashed to the ground, sprawling across the mouth of the driveway. The slender figure had been heading toward the tree line, but suddenly changed direction and ran toward the limb instead. The person was unaware of Lucky gaining at his heels.

Devil's forks plunged to earth around the pair with reckless abandon. They'd all be lucky if they weren't skewered by flying debris or electrocuted by lightning.

Rain hammered his bare skin, driving R.J.'s eyes nearly closed. He saw the figure begin to tug uselessly at the thick limb as Lucky caught up. Cursing under his breath, R.J. put on a burst of speed. By the time he reached them, the figure had backed against the fallen limb and was waving a large stick aggressively in Lucky's direction.

"Lucky! Sit!"

Not that he expected the dog to obey even if he'd heard the shouted order over the storm. Lucky wasn't real clear on commands. He knew what the words meant, he just wasn't convinced they applied to him.

Lucky barked. He cocked his head at the stick, as if trying to determine the rules of this new game. And the person was so intent on the dog that R.J. realized he'd gone unnoticed. As the person swung the stick at Lucky, R.J. reached out and intercepted the blow, wrenching the stick away. The person whirled to face this new threat as Lucky barked happily.

Not Valerie, but a woman nonetheless. Her fear-filled eyes were as wild as the storm.

"It's okay," he shouted to be heard over the storm. "He won't hurt you. We've got to get inside!"

"No!"

There wasn't time to argue. Energy sizzled in the air around them. Thunder bellowed and before she realized what he was going to do, he stepped forward and lifted her off her feet. She screamed and fought him as he slung her over his shoulder like a sack of wet cement.

Except cement would have been more cooperative. There wasn't an ounce of cooperation in this sodden woman. He had to pin her legs so she couldn't kick him, but there wasn't a thing he could do about the hands that pummeled his bare back.

Lucky barked his approval of this new and exciting game. Lightning momentarily blinded him as he hurried back up the drive with his burden. R.J. figured if they made it back inside without getting killed, it would be a miracle.

By the time he mounted the steps, he was breathing heavily. He opened the door, took four steps inside and dumped her on her feet. She scrambled away, stumbling in her haste. He ignored her to close and lock the door behind Lucky, who promptly began to shake the water free from his fur all over the hall.

"Lucky, no!" He made another grab for the animal's collar. "Not in here! Come on, we'll go to the mudroom…"

His voice tapered off as he found himself facing the business end of a small but lethal-looking gun.

"…or not."

She'd backed against the far wall. Her wide eyes had lost only a little of that frenzied wildness he had glimpsed outside.

Frustrated and more than a little annoyed, R.J. stared at the weapon in her hand. Even if he and Lucky had scared her half to death, the idea that she'd pull a gun on him in his own house made him angry.

"Put that thing away," he demanded.

She took a shuddery breath. "Not a chance."

As though finally sensing the dangerous atmosphere between the humans, Lucky plopped to a sitting position at R.J.'s feet, gazing between them with soulful eyes. His whine seemed to ask what had gone wrong.

"Stay where you are," she commanded.

With a quick shake of her own head, she tossed back long matted strands of hair, sending droplets of water flying much as Lucky had done.

The low-voiced contralto was husky and a bit shaky, but she was in control, which was a major relief. At least she wouldn't pull the trigger by accident.

She was a bedraggled sight with her sodden hair plastered to her head and face. Her jacket and jeans were sopping wet, as well. She reminded him of a drowned puppy. One with teeth, he decided, eyeing the gun.

"I'm not going to hurt you."

"You've got that right."

She had guts he'd give her that much.

"Look, I'm sorry if I scared you, but we couldn't stand around out there and you didn't look as though you were going to listen to reason."

"I said, don't move!"

He halted the step he'd started to take in her direction. She was scared. Scared people with guns were apt to do stupid things. Like shoot someone.

"Fine. I'm not moving. What are you doing here?"

He knew he sounded angry, but staring down the barrel of a gun seemed to have that effect on him.

"Trying to leave," she retorted.

"Great! Don't let me stop you."

Her eyes narrowed. "You just did."

"My mistake. Go." He waved a hand toward the door.

She glared as more of the wildness faded from her gaze.

"My car's stuck in the mud," she admitted reluctantly.

That figured. "Where?"

She raised her chin defiantly. "Under some trees at the side of your driveway. I need help getting it out."

He nodded at the gun. "You've got a strange way of asking for help, lady."

"You grabbed me," she pointed out. And she didn't lower the gun.

"It was hardly a thrill. You were about to get us all killed out there. Or maybe you didn't notice that lightning. It was practically coming down on top of us."

"I was trying to move that branch."

He stared at her, saw she was serious and shook his head. "You need a chainsaw."

"So help me."

"Not a chance, lady. I'm not suicidal. Take a look out there!"

A shiver ran through her. He decided she wasn't going to shoot him and gave her his best glare.

"And put that thing away before you hurt someone."

He took a step forward. Her hand tightened convulsively. Maybe she would shoot him after all. The fear was back in her eyes. He felt a twinge of guilt, but shook it aside.

"Look, I've had it with you. Either shoot me or don't, but I've got things to do. One of those lightning strikes took out the power. Now if holding that gun makes you feel more secure, feel free, but I have to go out back to start the generator."

R.J. suited action to words, moving with deliberate care as he started into the living room. She tensed. So did he, but the half-expected sound of a gunshot didn't come. He continued through the dining room and out to the kitchen, releasing his breath.

Lucky padded ahead, hoping for a treat. After a second, R.J. sensed her following them.

"Watch where you step," he cautioned gruffly without turning around. He paused to turn off the turbo fans as he went past so they wouldn't blare to life once he started the generator.

"Are you lost?" he asked without looking at her.

"Not if you're R.J. Monroe."

Chapter Two

R.J. spun around. He hadn't expected that. She took a hasty step back. Her hand was thrust inside her jacket pocket, holding the gun no doubt. She might be nervous but she faced him boldly.

"Who are you?"

"Stay where you are," she commanded.

"Please," he added with soft menace. She froze.

"What?"

"You aren't real big on manners, are you? 'Stay where you are, please.' My foster parents were sticklers for good manners," he explained. "They taught me a person gets a lot farther on a few please-and-thank-yous than all the bullying in the world."

Scowling, her voice deepened. "Please."

R.J. stopped moving. "Do you always abuse a person's hospitality this way?"

The sudden crack of thunder was so loud they both gave a start. For a second, R.J. was afraid she'd fired the gun. Lucky barked and shook himself again.

"Come here, dog."

Ignoring her and the possibility she'd shoot him, R.J. strode past her without another word. Lucky trotted after him into the mudroom. Drying the dog off gave him a chance to collect his thoughts. She knew his name, but he was pretty sure he'd never seen her before, and he couldn't imagine anyone being mad enough to send someone after him with a gun.

She came to the doorway, a silent shadow watching as he toweled Lucky and reached for the dog treats in the box up high on the shelf. The gun made him nervous. He had a feeling it wouldn't take much for one to go off in inexperienced hands, and she didn't look all that experienced to him.

Pulling a clean towel from the stack in the basket waiting to be carried upstairs, he set it on the dryer. "You can use this to dry off. I need to start the generator."

Without waiting for her reaction, he grabbed the flashlight and a jacket from the hook and stepped back outside into the storm. The worst of it seemed to be moving away.

R.J. debated his options. He could go around to the front and try to come in behind her and take the gun away, but that seemed risky. She could have shot him already if that had been her intent. And he was curious. Who was she? What *did* she want?

He wished he had thought to grab his cell phone. Then he could have called Wyatt. As Stony Ridge's chief of police, Wyatt Crossley could have told him the best way to handle this situation. Even better, he would have sent reinforcements to take the crazy lady off R.J.'s hands.

He ran around the side of the house and started down the drive. There was still too much lightning in the air for comfort, but he spotted the glint of chrome after a brilliant flash that wasn't as close as most had been. The small car was mired in the mud under the trees all right. Well and truly stuck.

Texas plates. He whistled under his breath. She was a long way from Texas. And he didn't know anyone from that part of the country. What was this all about? The car was locked. A purse and a pair of night-vision goggles sat on the front seat.

Not exactly standard equipment for any of the women he knew. There was also a blanket and pillow on the back seat and a tidy bag of what looked like trash on the floor.

Now why would a woman come lóoking for him with a gun and a pair of night-vision goggles? This made no sense, but there was only one way to get any answers. He hurried back around the house and got the generator started. For once, it purred to life without argument.

The mudroom was empty as he stepped back inside. Her jacket dripped from a hook. Nice to see she was making herself at home. He hung his beside it and checked her pocket.

"I kept the gun," she told him.

"Figured as much."

Unrepentant, he turned. Suddenly he was aware that his chest was bare and dripping wet. She'd used the towel to wrap her hair turban-style, but the black, long-sleeved turtleneck she'd worn under her jacket was nearly as wet as her coat. Wet enough to cling like a second skin, outlining lush curves. There were dark circles under her eyes. She looked exhausted.

He turned to the clothes dryer. He did not want to feel sorry for her. He wanted to cling to his anger, but something about her made that difficult. Pulling out a black T-shirt and a pair of sweatpants, he glanced up at her.

"I have extras if you want something dry to wear. They'll be big, but better than wet clothes."

"I have a suitcase in my car," she told him.

"Good. When the storm stops, you can get it."

She frowned, watching as he used another towel to dry his hair and pat his chest dry.

"I'm about to drop my pants, so unless you want the full show, you might want to step back in the kitchen."

The air charged with electricity more potent than the sky outside. Color suffused her cheeks. Without a word, she backed out of sight. R.J. grinned and stripped quickly, toweling himself thoroughly before donning the clean outfit.

She wasn't beautiful, though she was pretty in a wholesome sort of way that definitely didn't go with the gun. And while she intrigued him, he was in no mood to play games with strangers, pretty or otherwise.

He tugged his softball sweatshirt off the hook and found her standing in the middle of the kitchen, next to Lucky, looking lost.

"Here. You look cold. It's not freshly laundered like the stuff in the dryer, but it's warm." Hesitantly, she accepted the sweatshirt. "There's a bathroom off the kitchen that backs to this laundry room."

"I know."

So she'd done some exploring while he'd been outside. "Looking for more weapons?"

"Do you have some?"

Under other circumstances, he would have come back with a teasing rejoinder, but tonight he was all out of humor.

"If you decide to change, you can throw your wet stuff in the dryer," he told her gruffly.

She didn't reply and he couldn't tell what she was thinking.

"Have you eaten?" he asked.

"I'm fine."

"Suit yourself."

He crossed to the gas stove and put the kettle on. A powerful gust of wind shook the old farmhouse. Aware of her standing there looking a bit uncertain, he pulled out a box of vanilla wafers. Instantly, Lucky appeared at his side.

"These aren't for you, dog."

His stubby tail wagged and Lucky offered a wide doggy grin. Before the woman even moved, R.J. sensed she'd made up her mind. Without a word, she went back into the laundry room and he heard the dryer open.

Satisfied, he relaxed and put the cookies on a plate. Then he set about preparing a couple of mugs of hot chocolate. Barefoot, he padded into the living room, mindful of the littered floor. After starting a fire in the fireplace, he set up a couple of TV trays. Lucky stayed with him, hoping a cookie or two might find their way to the floor.

"All you think about is your stomach, dog."

Lucky woofed agreement. R.J. was aware that the woman had gone into the bathroom. He carried the mugs of chocolate into the living room and waited. A few minutes later, he heard her start the clothes dryer.

"I hope you like marshmallows in your chocolate," he said when she came in, surveyed the room and perched uneasily on the edge of the couch across from him. The couch was closer to the fireplace. He figured she probably needed the warmth it would offer once the fire caught properly.

She wore a pair of his sweatpants beneath his old sweatshirt. He assumed she'd donned the clean T-shirt as well. She really did look exhausted. And ill at ease.

"What did you do with the gun?"

Her hand automatically went to her waist. "Why?"

"I like to keep track of things like guns in my house, lady. Lucky's a gentle animal, but he takes a dim view of anyone trying to harm the person who fills his food bowl."

Lucky gazed up at him hopefully, tongue lolling. Her color heightened, but she didn't apologize. He sort of liked that about her.

"Stop calling me lady."

"Fine. Give me a name."

"Teri."

"Just Teri?"

"For now."

And he sort of liked that, as well. She might be tired and scared, but she wasn't going to let him intimidate her.

"Okay. We've established that I'm R.J. Monroe and you came here to see me. I'm guessing you don't want your house redone in the middle of the night, so what can I do for you?"

TERI HESITATED a second before meeting his gaze. She had the strongest urge to tell him she was Corey's aunt and all she wanted was her nephew. But the sense of suppressed violence in him stilled the words.

"Tell me what you did with Valerie and Corey," she demanded instead.

R.J. paused in the act of lifting a cookie. Of all the things he'd expected her to say, apparently, that hadn't been one of them.

"What does a woman from Texas want with Valerie and her son?" he asked slowly.

A flare of panic turned her hot, then cold. "How do you know I'm from Texas?"

"License plate on your car."

So that was what had taken him so long outside. It hadn't occurred to her that he'd check out her car, but she'd locked it. She was pretty sure she'd locked it. So she told herself it didn't matter and lifted her chin.

"Where are they?"

"Why should I tell you?"

She decided she didn't like him. He was too handsome, too arrogant and more than a little intimidating. And he knew it, too. He was deliberately baiting her. On the other hand, she needed his cooperation.

"We don't have time for games, Mr. Monroe. I'm a private investigator. Lester Boyington knows his wife came here to meet you. He found your e-mail about Heartskeep."

Watching him closely, she saw his jaw harden as his body tensed.

"If he gets to her," she added firmly, "he'll kill her."

He tossed the uneaten cookie to Lucky who snapped it out of the air and waited hopefully for more.

The man didn't look at the animal. His gaze remained fastened on hers. It took real effort not to squirm under that steady stare.

"And you know this because...?"

Anger made her snap at him. "Because I broke into their house early this morning and found your e-mail on their computer. I half hoped it was a false trail she'd laid for Lester to follow. But it wasn't, was it?"

"You broke into their house?"

She shouldn't have told him that, yet it didn't seem to shock him. He probably figured investigators did things like that every day. Still, she picked her next words with more care.

"I'd been watching the house since dawn. When I

was certain Lester wasn't inside, I went in to get them out but they were already gone. Valerie had left the computer on—or someone had. Your message was on the screen."

R.J. swore. His expression was angry enough to send her hand toward her waistband.

"Why were you trying to get them out?"

"Because Lester Boyington is dangerous."

He studied her expression as if trying to read her mind.

"Who are you, Teri?"

Her eyes flicked away from his gaze afraid he'd see the lie. "I told you, I'm a private investigator. My name's Teri Johnson."

"Let me see your license."

She set her jaw. "It's in my purse and as you've already seen, that's in the car."

"Who are you working for?"

She was on safer ground now. "That's privileged information."

"Consider me privileged, then."

"I don't think so."

He seemed to grow larger and even more menacing as he straightened in his chair. She'd already seen the strength of those work-hardened muscles and once again she was conscious of how isolated they were in this old farmhouse. Not to mention how unprepared she was to deal with a man like this. She couldn't afford to show a single sign of weakness.

"Where's Valerie?" she forced herself to demand once more.

The expression that flitted across his features came and went too fast for her to categorize. His eyes narrowed.

"Do you know Valerie?"

She hesitated. "I know she's in danger. I need to get to her."

She should have said yes. What was one more lie? He considered her for a long, lingering moment.

"Valerie told me she had no one else to turn to. Yet you claim you came to rescue her."

Teri clamped her mouth shut. What could she say unless she told him the truth?

"How do I know you aren't working for her husband?"

"Never!"

He seemed momentarily startled by her vehemence.

"So you don't know Valerie, but you do know her husband."

Dark anger stirred. Her stomach clenched. She didn't lower her gaze. She willed him to listen and believe.

"I know that men who get off on hurting women, children or animals should be tortured, castrated and imprisoned for the rest of their natural lives."

R.J. blinked and sat back. His brow furrowed as he studied her.

"Tell me where Valerie is," she pressed.

He scowled while his jaw clenched with some dark emotion. "I wish I knew."

"What's that supposed to mean?"

"Valerie disappeared from Heartskeep sometime last night."

Teri closed her eyes as defeat washed over her. She was too late. Again. Bleakly she opened her eyes and regarded him.

"Lester got to them?"

"We don't know what happened." His voice roughened. "The police found her cell phone crushed behind the house near the fountain. Her car, all her belongings, everything was still there, except her."

Her heart pounded faster. "What about Corey?"

To her surprise, R.J.'s features gentled. "The boy's fine. Valerie left everything behind, including her son."

It was on the tip of her tongue to protest that Valerie wasn't Corey's mother. She stopped the words in time, but it rankled all the same. Still, Lester hadn't gotten Corey.

The jolt of hope was tempered by questions. "Why would Lester take Valerie and not Corey?"

Could Valerie still be alive?

"We don't know that anyone did take her. It's possible she left on her own."

"Right. After crushing her cell phone."

To her surprise, a hint of embarrassed color washed his face.

"It's possible."

Anything was possible. Maybe Teri hadn't been too late after all. Maybe Valerie had sought asylum at Heartskeep in order to leave Corey behind so she could continue to run unhampered by a young child. She could have crushed the cell phone herself in an effort to point the police in Lester's direction.

Staring at his troubled expression, Teri decided R.J. didn't have the answers she needed.

"This Heartskeep place is a woman's shelter, right?"

He nodded.

"Can you take me there?" If he noticed the edge of demand in her voice, it didn't seem to bother him.

"At the moment? No."

"In the morning, then." But she let her dissatisfaction show.

"Valerie is gone, Teri."

But Corey wasn't. "She may come back."

"For Corey," he agreed. "I can't see her leaving her son behind."

She swallowed a retort. "Doesn't Heartskeep have safety precautions in place to protect the women?"

"Of course it does. For one thing, there's a high fence around the perimeter of the estate."

She snorted. "Fences can be climbed."

"Not this one. And the house is wired with an alarm system."

She dismissed the alarm with a wave of her hand. "No cameras? No guard dogs?"

"It's a woman's shelter, not a prison."

"Well, someone must have seen something."

"The police have questioned everyone." He rubbed his jaw in frustration. "No one knows what happened. Valerie simply disappeared sometime after she went to her room last night. We spent most of the day searching the grounds. Heartskeep has umpteen acres of ground to cover and a lot of it is wooded. Despite that, there should have been some sign somewhere if she didn't leave under her own power, and there wasn't. Except for the cell phone."

Wearily, Teri leaned back against the couch and closed her eyes. He could be lying, but she didn't think he was.

"It doesn't make sense."

"Tell me about it," he agreed.

When she opened her eyes again, he was studying her with a masculine expression that made her distinctly uneasy. Self-consciously, she pushed at a strand of hair slipping out from under the towel.

"Have they asked her husband what happened?"

"They have to find him first."

"He's...not at home?" she corrected, changing the tone to make it a question.

"Not according to the police in Maryland."

Her fingernails tapped restlessly against the steaming mug. Reflected firelight flickered across his features. His dark good looks stopped short of being to-die-for handsome, but R.J. projected an aura of self-confidence that would be irresistible to most women.

Teri scowled at him. "Will you please take me to Heartskeep?"

He picked up his mug and took a long swallow of the rapidly cooling chocolate. "Why?"

"So I can talk to the people who were there last night."

"You don't need me for that. All you have to do is go and ring the buzzer."

"But you know them. You could introduce me."

He set his mug down and regarded her with dark blue eyes that didn't seem to miss much. "I could, but I don't know you, do I?"

The towel slipped to one side. Thankful to have an outlet for her jumpy nerves, Teri released it and began to briskly rub the terry cloth over her wet hair. Exhaustion threatened to overtake her at any moment. The snapping heat of the fire and the calming warmth of the hot chocolate were conspiring against the need that had driven her this far. She was fading fast and she knew it.

"Why did you come here, Teri? Why didn't you go to the police and enlist their help instead of coming to me?"

She hoped he didn't see her flinch. She knew exactly how much help she'd get from the authorities if she told them who she really was. She thought about her sister lying in that hospital bed in a deep coma from which she might never awaken and set her jaw.

If Lester even had a suspicion that she and her sister were still alive, he wouldn't rest until he finished what he'd started, and no one would be able to stop him.

A gust of wind shook the house, rattling windows. Abruptly, R.J. set his cup down and stood. Her gaze flashed to his face.

"I'm going to assume we're on the same side for now, Teri, but I've been up since four-thirty this morning and tomorrow promises to be another bad day. I have to be up again in a few hours, so let me have your gun and you can spend the night."

She straightened, coming wide awake. "Not a chance."

"This isn't negotiable."

"Forget it."

"How do I know you won't shoot me in my sleep?"

"How do I know you won't attack me in mine?" she fired back.

"I'd say a little trust is called for here."

"Yeah? How little?"

Maybe if she hadn't been so tired she would have been quicker. Then again, probably not. R.J. was incredibly fast. He was across the room in the blink of an eye with her wrists pinned before she could move. Using his weight and strength, he pushed her down into the back of the couch.

Lucky barked sharply as she thrashed, kicking at him, but she'd taken off her shoes. Fear-fed adrenaline surged through her as one hand went to the waistband of her slacks.

As suddenly as it had begun, the attack was over. He released her and stepped back holding the gun. Teri surged to her feet in front of him quivering in rage and fear.

"Sorry," he told her without a trace of contriteness. "My house, my rules."

He opened the cylinder and dropped the shells into the palm of his hand. Tossing them on the couch beside her, he held her gaze.

"You keep the bullets. I'll keep the gun."

Shock, fear and anger mixed together in her mind.

"For what it's worth, Teri, if I'd wanted to attack you, I'd have done so. I prefer a willing partner."

"Bastard!"

"I've been called worse."

Lucky whined at their feet, obviously upset by the tension in the room. R.J. shoved the gun into his pocket and rested his hand on the dog's large head in a reassuring gesture.

"Feel free to leave if you want, but if you do go out to your car, you won't be coming back inside tonight."

The hard-edged words were a promise rather than a threat. Teri believed him. As shaken as she was, part of her understood. He had no reason to trust her and no way to know whether she had another weapon in the car.

"I don't have a spare bed," he continued. "But the couch isn't bad. I've slept on it myself on occasion. And it's better than your car. Warmer, for one thing. I'll get you some blankets and a pillow while you make up your mind."

Arrogant bastard.

Lucky trotted beside him as he strode from the room. Badly shaken, she rubbed at her wrists where he had grabbed them in that steely vise. He was even stronger than he looked. He could have easily hurt her if that had been his intent. Yet he hadn't.

Stay or go?

Teri dropped down on the edge of the couch. What choice did she have? The bottom line was that she needed R.J. if she wanted to get to Corey. It might be too late to help Valerie, but Corey was still here.

But why? Why hadn't Lester taken him away?

Slowly, she made her way to the tiny bathroom behind his laundry room. Dark smudges of exhaustion underscored the brilliant green color of her eyes. The hue seemed far too bright and out of place against the stark whiteness of her skin. She gazed at her reflection in the chipped mirror over the old-fashioned sink and conceded her stupidity.

She shouldn't have come here tonight. She should have waited for morning. Now she was stuck here with a man she didn't like. A man who scared the heck out of her in more ways than one.

She was too tired and too shaken to think straight anymore. Stealthily, she slipped into the kitchen and removed a steak knife from the wooden holder on the counter. Feeling only slightly foolish, she carried the knife with her into the bathroom. If her instincts turned out to be wrong about him, at least now R.J. Monroe wasn't going to find her totally unarmed and defenseless.

FOR A MINUTE, R.J. thought she'd run after all. He dumped the linens on the couch and started for the door, only stopping when he heard water running in the downstairs bathroom. He relaxed, not sure whether to be pleased or not. He probably wouldn't sleep a wink with Teri under his roof, but his choices were limited.

Besides, guilt gnawed at him. He'd been unduly rough with her. Her terrified expression when he'd grabbed her was going to haunt him for a long time to come. On the other hand, she'd already pointed that gun at him once tonight and he wasn't going to apologize for taking it away.

Who was she working for? Why keep her client's identity a secret unless she was helping the husband? But R.J. couldn't bring himself to believe that she was. There had been an intensity in her voiced dislike of Lester Boyington that rang true.

Unless she was a good actress, simply pretending.

After making up the couch, R.J. tidied the room, filled and set the automatic coffeepot to drip at the usual hour and added wood to the fire. He was too tired to puzzle out the mystery of his strange houseguest tonight.

Lucky sprawled outside the bathroom door waiting for her. R.J. had a hunch she wouldn't come out until she heard him go back up the stairs.

"Guard her, Lucky," he told the dog loudly enough for her to hear if she was listening.

Lucky's stubby tail whomped the floor. Teri didn't know it yet, but her biggest danger was in being licked to death.

It was going to be a very long night.

Chapter Three

Morning brought a thick layer of fog and an uneasy truce. R.J. hadn't expected to sleep at all, let alone so deeply, but the stresses of the day before had taken their toll and he'd awoken at his normal time, surprised that Lucky wasn't there nudging him awake.

At least she hadn't murdered him in his bed.

Despite the early hour, she was dressed again in her own clothes when he got downstairs and Lucky was barking to be let back inside. He fed the dog while Teri poured coffee for them both. She diluted hers with plenty of milk and sugar, he noted.

"Have a seat while I make us some eggs," he told her. "Scrambled, okay? With cheese? I've tried doing them over easy but they usually end up scrambled anyway."

"I don't eat breakfast." Her stomach growled loudly in protest.

R.J. raised his eyebrows, noting the way her blush gave her high cheekbones a delicate pink stain. She really was quite attractive. He wondered what she'd look like in something other than black.

Though obviously embarrassed, she held his gaze. "I didn't have dinner last night. Scrambled eggs would taste great."

He wanted to smile but didn't. "I've got precooked bacon strips, too. They aren't as good as the real deal, but I don't have much time most mornings."

"That's okay. Eggs are more than enough. What can I do to help?"

"How are you at toast?"

"Depends on the toaster."

"Not the domestic sort, huh?"

"There are restaurants for a reason, you know."

He didn't want to like her, but she made it difficult. He found his guard slipping as they prepared breakfast with the deft ease of people who had done so together more than once. The domesticity of the scene unsettled him. R.J. was fully conscious of her on several levels, and that alone was disturbing. Letting himself be attracted to her wasn't smart. He needed to keep in mind that the woman was here with an agenda.

"Where's the army that's going to help us eat all this?" she asked, watching him stir the grated cheese into a huge mound of eggs in the frying pan.

"I work construction. I protein and carbo-load most mornings. You should see what I have for lunch."

Her lips quirked. "Pass."

"You one of those women who diet all the time?"

"No."

That had struck an unexpected nerve. Her flat tone and severe expression left him wondering, but then he should have known better than to mention the *D* word to a woman.

She set silverware on his small table, poured them each a glass of apple juice and, at his request, buttered several slices of toast.

"Are you always this domestic?" she asked as they sat down together.

"Not much choice if I want to eat. You'll have noticed there aren't a lot of restaurants nearby."

Lucky plopped on the floor between them with his usual wistful expression.

"Your dish is over there," R.J. reminded him. But he broke off a slice of bacon and tossed it to the dog. For a second, he thought Teri was going to scold him, but she reconsidered and started eating.

For someone who didn't eat breakfast, she made hearty inroads on the food he'd put in front of her, including the bacon strips. She could stand to gain a few pounds, though he wouldn't have told her so under torture.

She was a little too thin, if generously proportioned. Her dark red hair floated around a pinched face that still showed lines of strain. She'd made an effort to restrain the silken mass of her hair, but his bathroom wasn't well equipped for unexpected guests. Probably because he rarely had any. At least the smudges beneath her impossibly green eyes weren't as dark as they had been last night, but the sliding glances she kept sending his way were still wary.

Fine with him. R.J. didn't trust her, either.

"Sleep okay?"

Startled, she looked up. "Yes. Thank you. But your dog licked me awake before the crack of dawn. He made it clear he wanted out, so I turned him loose. Hope that was okay."

"Absolutely. I appreciate it. Lucky's a dog of simple needs, but he does think people are here to serve."

"Uh-huh. Well, if you ever run out of sandpaper, I'm sure his tongue could fill in for you in a pinch."

R.J.'s lips curved. The persistent tug of sensual awareness annoyed him. He decided it had been too long since his last date and finished his meal quickly, anxious to clear his driveway and get her car out of the mud. He'd be glad to send her on her way. The thing was, he had a feeling it wasn't going to be that easy.

He was right.

"Do you think we could make a fresh start this morning?" she asked over a forkful of eggs.

"In what way?"

"Tell me everything you know about the night Valerie disappeared."

His fingers tightened around his coffee mug. He took a swallow to buy some time. He couldn't see any reason not to share the small amount of information he had. He'd already told her most of it anyhow.

"According to Kathy Walsh—she's the house mother, I guess you'd call her. Anyhow, according to Kathy, Valerie went to her room shortly before eleven. In the morning, she was gone. Her son and her clothes and her car were still there. Even her purse. She wasn't."

He found he was gripping the cup tightly enough to snap the handle and set it down. Teri's expression was equally bleak.

"No one heard a thing. The house alarm was still armed for the night. All the doors and windows were locked. One of the kids heard her son crying that morning and Kathy went up to check on them."

A flash of sympathy, almost pain, came and went in her expressive, too green eyes.

"The chief of police is a friend of mine. Wyatt's wife is the founder of the shelter so he was called in right away. He discovered the broken cell phone in back by the fountain," he went on more calmly. "Wyatt thinks it belonged to Valerie, but he's checking to confirm that. He came to see me right after he found the phone."

"Why?"

There was no need to tell her how Wyatt had questioned him about R.J.'s argument with Valerie the evening she disappeared. Wyatt had only been doing his job. And quite possibly that argument *was* responsible for her disappearance. If he hadn't pressured her to talk to Wyatt and press charges against her husband, maybe she wouldn't have run.

"I took her to Heartskeep. Wyatt thought maybe I knew where she had gone."

Mistrust was back in Teri's eyes. R.J. ignored it and continued.

"We searched the grounds until it got too dark to see. By then, it was raining hard enough to wash away any useful evidence of anything. The thing is, if she'd stayed close to the house someone would have found her."

"Why would she have gone outside in the first place?"

R.J. raised and dropped his shoulders. "We don't know. It's possible she went to get something from her car before the house alarm was turned on and surprised someone on the grounds, possibly an intruder who had nothing to do with her husband. The crushed cell phone was found in some disturbed grass out in the maze. That's quite a distance from the parking area and there were no signs of a struggle near the car, nor that anyone had been dragged there. I can't come up with a single reason for her to have gone into the maze that night. It was dark and raining."

Feeling the helpless anger once more, he had to force his tightly balled fingers to relax.

"Maybe she ran from someone and was trying to use the cell phone to call for help," Teri suggested.

"Or she dropped it when she was unloading things from her car and someone else took the phone out back."

"And crushed it?"

R.J. shrugged again. "I agree it's unlikely, but we have no idea what happened. She simply vanished."

Teri wasn't sure what to make of the undercurrent of anger in his voice, but the suppressed violence set her stomach churning. She'd seen how strong he was.

But if he'd hurt Valerie, would he be angry? She didn't think so. The problem was, she no longer trusted her instincts when it came to men.

"How is it you know Valerie?" Had they been lovers?

"Her brother was one of my best friends in high school. Valerie used to tag along after us like a puppy."

Or a girl with a crush? Teri didn't voice that aloud but it seemed likely. A lot of women would be drawn to R.J.'s good looks and self-confidence.

"Valerie has a brother?"

"I thought you were a private investigator."

"There wasn't time to run a background check on her," she told him quickly. "My job was to find her and offer her protection from her husband."

"Who hired you?"

"I told you, I'm not at liberty to say."

Those dark blue eyes turned frosty. Teri worked to control a shiver, but she refused to be intimidated by him.

"You'd better get permission, then," he said softly, "because Wyatt isn't going to accept that answer."

"The police can't force me to answer questions."

"Don't bet on it."

She hoped he couldn't tell how the softly spoken threat had unnerved her.

"Why did she e-mail you in the first place? Were you her lover?"

The last part came out before she could stop the question. Only a flick of his eyes revealed any emotion at all. She couldn't tell what he was thinking, but she wished she hadn't asked.

"How long have you been a private investigator?"

She raised her chin defiantly. "Long enough to know when I'm being stonewalled. If you're her *friend*, you'll help me."

"Will I?"

Trust came hard, but if she wanted his help she knew she was going to have to bend a little. "We could sit here glaring at each other all day, but it wouldn't solve a thing. I came here to offer Valerie and Corey a safe refuge from Lester."

"What sort of safe refuge?"

Exasperated, she set down her fork and pushed aside her plate. "If I told you that, it wouldn't be safe."

"You think I'd hurt her?" he demanded.

"I don't know you, do I?" she replied, mimicking his earlier words to her.

His eyes narrowed. "You could be working for her husband."

"And you could be the person she met out by the fountain," she countered.

His penetrating gaze would unnerve most people. She was far from immune, but Teri forced herself to hold his gaze steadily, even though her heart thudded against her chest.

Without comment, he set her gun on the table and stood, carrying his dishes to the sink. For a moment, Teri was stunned. The relief hit her hard. Her fingers trembled as she picked up the gun and tucked it into her waistband. Without a word, she gathered her dishes and joined him at the sink.

"What made you decide in my favor?"

"Who said I have?"

They proceeded to neaten the kitchen in silence while she seethed. He was the most arrogant, annoying man. Then she saw an answering anger simmering in his gaze.

"So why did you give me back my gun if you don't trust me?"

"Stupidity. On the other hand, I can always take it back from you if you try anything."

Arrogant, obnoxious… "You think so?"

"We both know so."

She wondered if she should have kept the steak knife instead of replacing it this morning. Lucky watched them anxiously, sensing the tension in the air. Teri swallowed down a hot reply. She needed R.J.'s help, not his anger. But the man did know how to infuriate her.

"I'm pretty sure her husband knows she came here, R.J."

"So you said."

"I also think he followed her here. I think he got to her the other night."

That made him pause. "How?"

"The same way I did. Your e-mail message. Your name, Stony Ridge and Heartskeep were all mentioned."

"I meant, how do you think he got to her?"

"Isn't it obvious? He called her cell phone."

R.J. didn't respond.

"Look, Lester won't be satisfied with hurting Valerie. He's going to come after you next for helping her."

"I sincerely hope so."

His expression clearly said he'd relish the idea.

"You're a fool. I may not have done my research on Valerie, but I did on Lester. The man is dangerous."

R.J.'s expression hardened. "I can be dangerous, too."

The hairs on the back of her neck raised. She didn't doubt his words. There was a core of steel in his tone. Just maybe he'd be a match for Lester.

"Earlier you said you broke into their house?"

She shifted at that steady stare. "Not exactly."

"What…exactly?"

Teri released a breath and reminded herself that she needed his trust. "I let myself in through an unlocked window. But that's not the point. I think Lester killed her."

For a long minute, R.J. didn't move. He didn't speak, but his features clearly showed a starkly dangerous side to the man. Then his normal expression settled into place.

"That's a strong statement."

She managed not to shudder. "Yes."

"Why would he kill her?"

Could she make him understand? Would it matter if he did?

"Lester is not what he appears to be. Most people who meet him will tell you he's one step from a halo."

"Murderer to saint is a pretty far leap."

She was no longer fooled by his mild tone. "Not as far as you might think. You haven't met him yet." She set her jaw, unwilling to get into a discussion about Lester Boyington. "Look, if you really care about Valerie, help me."

His eyebrows lifted. "How?"

"Take me to Heartskeep and introduce me to the people who were there."

"The police have already talked to everyone."

"Female officers?"

He didn't respond.

"These are women who've been abused, right? I can get them to tell me things they may not want to tell a male authority figure."

She knew R.J. didn't trust her, but he wanted Valerie found. If there was even a chance she could deliver, Teri felt sure he'd take the risk.

"And you think they'll tell a private investigator things they wouldn't tell Wyatt?"

"Maybe. I think it's worth a shot, don't you? Someone must have seen something."

"Not necessarily. It was dark. And you haven't seen Heartskeep."

"Then show me. Tell people I'm an acquaintance of yours."

"Who happens to be a private investigator?"

She met him glare for glare. His eyes fell first.

"Wyatt won't appreciate interference in his investigation."

The knot of tension in the pit of her stomach eased. He was going to help.

"Let me worry about your police chief."

He set the last dish in the dishwasher before answering. "I'll see about moving that branch from the driveway. Then we'll see if we can get your car out of the mud."

"I'll give you a hand."

"Ever use a chain saw?"

"Power tools don't scare me."

"What does?"

She met the challenge without flinching. She could have told him, but she didn't. And a few hours later, after she got her first glimpse of Heartskeep, Teri decided the huge old mansion might have to be added to her short list.

The wrought-iron gates that protected the vast grounds were intricately shaped, but, to her mind, dark and towering and intimidating. She waited in her mud-splattered car behind R.J.'s large truck while he spoke into the call box near the mouth of the gate. Then he punched a series of numbers into the box. After what seemed like a long wait, the gates slowly swung open.

If all it took was a pass code and R.J. had the code, he could have gotten inside whenever he wanted. So could anyone else. Or was it necessary to call first and be given a code? She didn't know much about security systems, but Valerie had gone missing so there was some way to beat them. Teri had no doubt that Lester had discovered that way.

The long, fog-cloaked driveway with its dripping trees was disturbing, but it did little to prepare a first-time-visitor for the impact of the house itself. The enormous structure squatted in the center of a clearing shrouded in mist. Dismally, its many windows reflected the gnarled, half-dressed trees and the bleak fall sky overhead.

"Welcome to Heartskeep," she muttered out loud.

If houses had souls, this one would be old and splotched with secrets.

Teri tried to quell her apprehension as she followed R.J. and Lucky onto the wide front porch. The imposing front door was unlocked. Because someone knew they were coming or did they leave it that way? Without knocking, RJ ushered her into a hall much too large for the purpose.

Though attempts had been made to make the insides cheerful with the use of colorful, welcoming fabrics, nothing could be done to shrink its overwhelming size. Heartskeep would never be a homey sort of place to anyone who wasn't fond of grand hotels.

The woman who bustled forward to greet them exuded the warmth the estate lacked. Kathy Walsh was probably in her midfifties. A slim, well-preserved woman with sad but friendly eyes, her expression showed concern and a trace of alarm.

"R.J., I'm so glad you came by. We have a bit of a situation. Alexis insisted on coming in this morning and now she's in labor. I've been trying to reach Wyatt, but either he turned off his cell phone or he's out of range. I don't want to call the dispatcher because at this point I'm not sure he'd have time to get here anyhow. Alexis needs to get to the hospital right away. Can you take us in your truck?"

"Of course."

R.J. strode into the enormous open room clearly visible from the front door. A group of women clustered around an attractive, very pregnant young woman bent over in a high-backed chair. She looked up ruefully as R.J. reached her.

"Wyatt told me to stay home today, but oh no, I just had to get some paperwork done. I felt fine other than a slight backache this morning. I had all kinds of energy when Will picked me up and drove me over here, but my water broke after he left to run an errand in town."

"Yeah, sometimes it happens that way," R.J. said calmly.

She smiled at him, shaking her head. "How would Stony Ridge's favorite bachelor know that?"

R.J.'s grin was cocky. "Television. A person can learn all sorts of things watching television."

"Yeah, well I hope you learned how to deliver a baby, because I'm not sure this one is going to wait much longer."

"He'll wait," R.J. promised. "Hear that, junior? Hang in there a little longer." He helped Alexis to her feet. "I'd offer to carry you, but Wyatt would probably punch me."

"Hah! You're just too much of a gentleman to point out you'd need a crane to lift me." She looked past him to where Teri had stepped forward to stand in the hall opening. "I'm sorry for the rude welcome. I'm Alexis Crossley."

"Teri Johnson. And no apology is needed," Teri told her. "There's nothing more incredible than the birth of a baby."

"True, but you'd think they could have come up with an easier system for giving birth to one."

Teri grinned, immediately warming to the woman.

"Let me grab my coat and I'll come with you," Kathy told R.J. She sent Teri a questioning look.

R.J. followed her gaze with a frown.

"Go ahead, R.J. I can wait here," Teri offered. She knew he wouldn't like it, but his truck wouldn't hold all of them.

The woman called Alexis doubled over again with a groan. That cinched the matter.

"Okay if Teri waits here with Lucky? She's not a guest."

"Fine," Kathy replied anxiously tugging on her jacket. "We need to go. Mrs. Norwhich is in the kitchen."

Teri grabbed Lucky by the collar so he wouldn't follow them. "Go."

R.J. shot a warning look in her direction and went.

Teri turned to the silent cluster of watching women and smiled. "Hi. I'm Teri. I'm a friend of R.J.'s."

"THE GHOST isn't going to like this," Boone whispered. His small face pleated with worry.

"It's okay, Boone," Nola consoled. "Ghosts don't hurt people."

Ian peered around the dim dining room as if making sure the ghost wasn't listening. "Haven't you ever heard of pol...pol...polter something or other?"

"Poltergeists," Nola told him briskly. "There's a book on them in the library. They throw things. But they don't make people disappear."

"Yeah? What about Corey's mom?" Ian demanded. "The ghost got her."

"Stop it," Nola ordered, laying an arm on her brother's thin shoulder. She felt him quiver and barely stopped a shiver herself. "You don't know that."

"Sure I do. I saw him. He was out by the fountain that night."

Nola did shiver this time. Her brother grabbed her hand. His fingers were cold in hers. The fountain was where the police had found the missing woman's cell phone all smashed. She'd heard them talking about it.

"You're making this up," she said.

"No, I'm not."

She could see he wasn't.

"And that isn't the best part," Ian added, his eyes growing large with suppressed excitement. "I heard two of the adults talking in the kitchen last night. I know who the blond ghost is and why he's haunting Heartskeep."

"Who?" she breathed.

Boone leaned in close as Ian lowered his voice still further.

"The man who used to live here before this house was turned into a place for people like us was a doctor. He murdered his wife and buried her in the maze. But first he hid all his money so no one could take it away from him." Ian paused for effect. "Then he went crazy. He got shot dead right on top of where he buried her."

Boone gripped his sister's hand so hard his fingernails punctured her skin. Nola pulled his bony shoulders more tightly against her body, holding him close as if she could fend off the feeling of horror licking at her mind, as well.

"It's still here, Nola," Ian pressed. "No one ever found his money because he's guarding it."

"You're making this up," she said again.

Ian's expression turned hurt. He drew back his head.

"Am not. Mrs. Walsh wasn't happy when Mrs. Isley asked about the story, but she admitted it was true. Even you have to admit Mrs. Walsh wouldn't lie."

No, it was unlikely the kindly Mrs. Walsh would tell a lie or a tall tale like that one.

"There's more," Ian added conspiratorially. "The house used to be different, with dark wood walls around the balconies upstairs. There were secret passages to get onto them. Only what if they didn't find all of the hidden passages, huh? I bet there are more. Look at all these dark walls."

He waved a hand expansively at the dark panels surrounding them and the others followed his gesture with wide eyes.

"I bet we could find them. I bet we could find the money and the ghost, too."

His words scared Nola. The idea was terrifying. And just a teeny, tiny bit appealing.

"That's stupid," she scoffed.

"Is not!"

"Ghosts don't need secret passages," Nola protested. "They can walk through walls."

Ian gave her a fierce scowl. "That doesn't mean they can't disappear inside one. I've been thinking about this. We saw the blond ghost disappear in this corner next to the fireplace, right? So what if there's a secret passage over here? We should look now while our moms are in the kitchen talking to that new woman."

Lucky nudged her arm for attention. Nola stroked the big dog's head absently. She was glad for his presence because Lucky wouldn't let anything bad happen. Nervously, she followed Ian to the gigantic fireplace that nearly spanned the back wall of the dining room.

"How are we going to find a secret passage even if there is one?" she asked.

"It's got to be the bookcase, like in the movies."

The three children eyed the bookcases that shored up either side of the big fireplace. Instead of books their shelves were filled with wine glasses and brightly colored dishes.

"If we break something, we're going to get in big trouble," Nola warned.

"We'll have to be careful, then. Move, Lucky."

"The ghost isn't going to like this," Boone warned unexpectedly, his small face seamed with worry.

"What ghost?"

All three children whirled at the sound of Teri's voice. She stepped into sight from the hall and offered them her most reassuring smile.

"Sorry. I didn't mean to scare you. I was looking for Lucky."

"You didn't scare me," the taller boy protested, recovering quickly.

"I'm glad. I'm Teri. You must be Ian. And you're Nola so this must be Boone. Your mothers were telling me about you."

Ian regarded her with a trace of belligerence. Boone peered up at her silently. The girl took her measure while resting a reassuring hand on her brother's arm. Lucky trotted forward, stubby tail wagging. Gratefully, Teri scratched him behind the ear.

"Thanks for keeping Lucky out of trouble while I was talking to your mothers. I'm a friend of R.J.'s. I told him I'd watch Lucky, but I got to talking and forgot about him."

"That's okay. Lucky likes us," Nola told her.

"I'm not surprised. Hanging with you guys would be a lot more fun than a group of boring adults. So you're looking for secret passages, huh? I bet a spooky old house like this one has all sorts of secrets."

The three children exchanged glances. As the oldest, Ian was obviously the spokesman.

"Heartskeep has lots of secrets," he agreed. "There used to be secret passages upstairs, but someone tore them down."

"Bummer. I'd love to find a secret room or see a ghost or two."

"You believe in ghosts?" Nola asked skeptically.

"I don't know," she answered honestly. "I've never seen one, but I think just about anything is possible, don't you?"

Ian eyed her suspiciously. "My mother says there's no such thing."

"She could be right. I like to keep an open mind."

"I've seen one," he announced boldly.

The children stared intently, waiting for her reaction.

"Was it scary?" she asked.

Lucky nudged her hand. Teri went back to petting him.

"I wasn't scared."

"Were too," Boone argued. Then he glanced at Teri and drew back, as if afraid he'd said something wrong.

Her heart hurt for the fearful child. This could be Corey in a few years if she wasn't successful in getting him away. Nola patted Boone's arm reassuringly in a motherly fashion that made Teri ache for her as well.

"I was not!" Ian bragged unfazed.

"Did I hear you say you saw the ghost the night the missing woman disappeared?" Teri interjected quickly.

Ian fell silent. His glance at Nola seemed to be asking her opinion.

"Ian says he did," Nola responded primly.

"I did!" he insisted hotly. "He was out back, near the fountain. That's where they found her cell phone, you know. It was all crushed and everything."

"Ian thinks the ghost took her," Nola put in, "but I told him ghosts don't hurt people."

Ian rounded on her. "How do you know?"

Teri stepped into the breach, fighting a wave of mingled fear and excitement.

"What did the ghost look like?"

The children fell silent. She'd let her tension come through and scared them. She had to go slower, win their trust.

"There are scientists who study ghosts, you know."

Three sets of eyes regarded her mutely.

"They have trouble because most adults never see one."

"I see him all the time," Ian bragged.

Nola pursed her lips but didn't argue.

"Will you tell me about him?" Teri asked.

Uncertainly, he looked at the others.

This was important. Teri knew Ian had seen something. Unfortunately, Betty Drexler chose that moment to appear in the doorway across from them.

"Mrs. Norwhich said lunch will be ready in about five minutes. The children need to go and wash their hands."

Teri tamped down her impatience as the children were ushered out to wash their hands. There was nothing she could do but go along to the kitchen with everyone else a few minutes later.

The women were still uneasy around her as they settled at the large table in front of yet another huge fireplace. Teri understood their mistrust all too well. They all had a good reason for caution, but it made things hard. She'd already discovered that none of them wanted to talk to her. They especially didn't want to answer any questions.

Two of the women were sporting obvious injuries. Ian's mother appeared to have the most physical damage. Her right arm was in a cast and a sling, and bruises mottled her face. Teri suspected there were more bruises hidden by her clothing.

She fought the burning rage and bitter helplessness that churned in her stomach when she looked at these women. Life was so unfair. But as the last person entered the dining room, she looked around with a sinking feeling.

"Where's Corey? I thought R.J. said only Valerie disappeared."

The women exchanged uneasy glances. It was the taciturn and rather eerie-looking Mrs. Norwhich who answered as she carried over a tureen of soup and placed it on the table.

"Wyatt had him placed in foster care yesterday."

Chapter Four

"Corey's gone? Who has him?"

The skeletal woman speared her with beady eyes. "You'd have to ask Wyatt." Turning, she ghosted back to the counter.

No one else met her eyes. If any of them knew the answer, they weren't going to tell her and she couldn't help wondering if R.J. had known Corey wasn't here. While he hadn't mentioned it, she hadn't put any special emphasis on Corey either. In fact, quite the opposite. She'd wanted him to think Valerie had been her priority.

Earlier, she'd asked to see the room Valerie had used. Mrs. Norwhich had given her a tight, suspicious look before shaking her tightly permed head.

"Room's locked. You'll have to ask Wyatt's permission to go inside."

Teri had no intention of talking with the chief of police if she could avoid it, so Ian was her only hope. While he also eyed her with suspicion, the boy was the most approachable person she'd met so far. Besides, she had a feeling he saw more than any of the adults sitting at the table. Somehow, she had to get him alone and convince him to talk to her.

Tension hovered like an uninvited guest over the meal. The women ate quickly or picked at their food. Even the children were subdued.

The groundskeeper joined the group late. Will Leftcowitz was a lean, tall man in his sixties. While pleasant and friendly enough, he said very little and looked at Teri with enough speculation to make her nervous. He ate quickly, excusing himself from the table the moment he finished.

Teri tasted nothing of the meal and didn't participate in what seemed to be the only safe topic of conversation, the coming birth of Alexis Crossley's baby. Even that subject seemed to make everyone uneasy with Teri in their midst. Valerie's disappearance must have left them feeling more vulnerable than ever. Teri saw no way to turn the conversation to what she really wanted to know.

Who had Corey?

She was relieved when the meal finished and the dishes were carried to the kitchen sink. Mrs. Norwhich waved them out, bustling peremptorily about the room. One of the women announced she was going to the library in search of something to read. The youngest of the group scurried for the back staircase without a word to anyone. Timid and plump, only her eyes spoke of inward scars.

Betty Drexler took her children to the playroom upstairs to complete an art project, but Ian begged off, saying he wanted to go to the library and find a book. His mother gave him a quick hug and excused herself to lie down for a while after promising to work with all the children in a couple of hours. Her haunted expression made Teri sick inside. Ian watched his mother leave with eyes far too old and serious for someone his age.

Aware that this was the perfect chance to talk with the boy, Teri smiled encouragingly at him. "Ian, would you be interested in doing some exploring before you go to the library?"

He hesitated before following her into the hall. "What sort of exploring?"

Teri lowered her voice. "We could look for that secret passageway."

Tilting his head, he seemed to be measuring how far to trust her. Lucky determined the issue by ambling to her side as if he belonged there. She stroked the dog's head, grateful for his support. At least the dog didn't view her as a potential enemy.

Ian lowered his voice to match hers. "Do you think I'm right?"

"I think it's worth having a look, don't you?"

He considered that carefully before nodding and leading her back inside the large dining room. He pointed toward the built-in bookcases that backed onto the kitchen wall.

"We were in the living room over there a few nights ago," he said indicating a pillar some distance away. "We saw the ghost walk in front of the fireplace and disappear."

"It was a man?" Teri asked.

"Uh-huh. He sort of looked like…like the man my mother married. I thought it was him at first until he walked to that corner right there and disappeared."

The pair of floor-to-ceiling cases that flanked the fireplace appeared to be solid maple and firmly attached to the walls. Without the lights from the overhead chandelier, the room was dark despite the skylight far overhead. The menacing gray sky cast a sinister pall over everything. Teri could see where the room would be a wall of blackness at night since there were no out-side windows.

"We waited and waited, but we never saw him again."

"Could he have walked around the corner into the other hallway?"

"No way. We would have seen him. Mrs. Walsh keeps a night-light on in the kitchen so there's always a little light in the hall. He just went in this corner and disappeared. I checked."

"You did?"

Ian nodded seriously. "Nola was scared. She was go-ing to go wake up her mother 'cause she thought some-one had gotten in the house. I told her all the doors were locked and the security system was on and everything. Mrs. Walsh said if we even opened a window, this loud alarm would sound and the police would come. He had to be a ghost, only Nola didn't believe me so I had to show her."

What had it taken for this small boy to do that? she wondered. He had to have been scared.

"I had my flashlight," he said as if reading her mind. "So I showed Nola that he'd disappeared. I even went and checked the hall to be sure."

She wanted to snatch the boy up and hug him close.

"You're braver than I would have been," she told him honestly.

Ian preened.

"But what if it *had* been an intruder, Ian? He could have hurt you."

The possibilities were terrifying. Lester was per-fectly capable of harming a child who got in his way.

"I would have run away and started yelling."

A desire to emphasize the danger warred with her

need to earn his trust. She compromised by deciding to tell R.J. about Ian's nocturnal wanderings. Maybe Ian would listen to R.J.

"What did the ghost look like? You said he looked like your stepfather."

Ian shrugged, obviously uncomfortable. "He looks like a man, you know. We call him the blond ghost."

She drew a shallow breath. Lester was blond. The possibility that he'd been prowling through this house filled her with dread. Because despite her assertion to the contrary, Teri didn't believe for a minute that the children had seen a real ghost. That meant someone had been creeping around the house late at night.

Lucky padded away from them as Ian walked to the corner. Teri studied the built-in shelves uneasily, wishing she had her flashlight. It was in the car with her other gear, and she didn't want to take the time to get it. There was no telling how long they would have to explore before someone came looking for Ian.

"There's no sign of hinges," she told the boy. "And not much room for the case to swing out."

"Maybe if we move some of the dishes or something."

"Maybe," she agreed doubtfully.

"What are you looking for?"

Teri and Ian turned guiltily at the sound of R.J.'s voice. Rain had flattened his dark, wavy hair and darkened his pants where his jacket must have ended. She was startled anew by his size and the easy confidence he projected. He was far too attractive for comfort as he stood there, his hand resting on Lucky's dark head.

"We're looking for secret passages," Ian told him eagerly.

R.J. frowned. "What makes you think there are secret passages in here?"

"This is where the ghost disappeared."

R.J. looked at Teri. She let her shoulders lift ever so slightly. Ian, however, was more than willing to tell R.J. about the night they'd seen the ghost disappear in this corner. Rather than looking upset, R.J. seemed more annoyed than concerned.

"You're a sharp guy, Ian. The bad news is, you didn't see a ghost. The good news is, the man you saw wasn't a stranger and you're right about a secret passage here in the corner."

"I am?" he breathed.

"He is?"

R.J. nodded. "If you promise not to tell, I'll show you."

"I promise," Ian whispered.

The lever that operated the moving shelf was so cleverly concealed, Teri was certain she never would have found it. The shelves didn't swing out, they slid behind to reveal a narrow opening.

R.J. stepped inside and flicked a switch. A bare lightbulb overhead revealed a set of narrow stairs leading up into darkness. Beyond the steps appeared to be a storage room.

"What is this place?" Teri asked, stepping inside behind Ian.

"I don't know what it was used for originally, but Kathy and Mrs. Norwhich use it to store all sorts of things, like the vacuum cleaner, mops, china and silver. There's even a wine rack over here."

"Wow," Ian breathed, moving forward, his eyes taking in everything. "Where do the stairs go?"

"They run alongside the back staircase and come out next to it on the wall upstairs. There's another exit across the room that opens into the kitchen pantry."

Ian watched avidly as R.J. showed him. A unit of shelves in the pantry moved aside soundlessly to allow a person inside the walk-in pantry.

"Awesome! This is so cool," Ian said excitedly. "Wait 'til I tell Nora and Boone." His expression suddenly turned worried. "But if we didn't see a ghost—"

"You saw Mr. Leftcowitz," R.J. told him.

Ian shook his head. "Mr. Leftcowitz has white hair. The ghost is a blond."

"White and blond look pretty much the same in the dark, don't you think?"

Ian frowned, clearly unconvinced. "Maybe."

"I thought Mr. Leftcowitz went home at night," Teri said, remembering something one of the women had said earlier.

"Most of the time he does, but once in a while he stays late to help Mrs. Walsh."

"He likes her," Ian put in. "I saw them kissing once."

R.J. blinked in surprise. "Well, what do you know about that? I'm glad to hear it. Mrs. Walsh deserves a nice guy like Will."

"So there's no ghost?" Teri asked.

"Not that I've ever seen and I've been hanging around Heartskeep for a couple of years now," R.J. told them. "There are a few cold spots and plenty of noises, but it's a drafty old place so that's only to be expected. Now look, Ian, this isn't a play area. I know how tempting it will be for you guys to sneak in here, but there's a lot of breakable stuff. You can't use this space, all right?"

His face fell. "All right. Are there other hidden rooms like this one?"

"There used to be. Mrs. Crossley had me tear them down."

"But no one ever found the money, right?"

"What money?"

"The money the doctor hid before he was killed."

R.J. tensed. "Who told you about that?"

"I heard Mrs. Isley ask Mrs. Walsh about him."

R.J. shook his head. "I don't know what you heard, but Dr. Thomas didn't have any money when he was killed. He paid it all out in blackmail. He wasn't a nice person."

From what sounded like a long way off they heard Betty Drexler calling Ian.

"More math," he groused.

R.J. grinned. "Yeah, it's a pain, but it's one of those things you have to know how to do. I use math every single day in my work. I bet a smart kid like you will catch on lots faster than I did. You'd better go. Remember, this place is off-limits."

"All right. Coming, Mrs. Drexler."

Teri was grateful to leave the gloomy hole-in-the-wall. She waited until the bookcase closed before regarding R.J.

"Do you really think Ian and the others saw Mr. Leftcowitz?"

"No," he admitted, no longer smiling. "I know they didn't."

Teri's eyes widened.

R.J. looked around and decided the dining room was too exposed for explanations.

"Come with me."

He led her to the spare bedroom directly across the hall from the dining room.

Her pace was wary. So were her eyes. R.J. left the bedroom door open and lowered his voice.

"I suspect Ian saw Jacob, not Will."

"Who's Jacob?"

"The relationship's a bit tenuous, but Alexis and her two sisters treat him as if he's their stepbrother. Jacob's mother was a nurse who worked for their stepfather. Jacob grew up here at Heartskeep and he's got blond hair."

"Why didn't you tell Ian that?"

"Because I don't want Alexis to find out he's been hanging around here. Jacob and Will are planning a computer center and a video arcade area in the basement as a surprise. Alexis is devoted to making this shelter a success and for reasons I won't go into right now, Jacob feels he owes Alexis and her sisters. He's a computer whiz and Will is a retired architect. They're trying to come up with a design for the space. As you can imagine, the basement is huge and at the moment it's nothing more than an empty cave."

"I thought you were a contractor. Why aren't you helping them?"

"I've been swamped with projects I've already committed to doing. My part will come once they establish a plan. I'll go over it with them and then bring in the crew to do the actual work. Kathy knows and I'm sure Mrs. Norwhich does, as well. Not much slips past her. But the fewer people who do know, the less chance someone will let it slip in front of Alexis or one of her sisters. The goal is to keep the project a secret as long as possible."

Suspicion darkened her eyes. "So this Jacob person has free access to the house and grounds?"

The question was completely reasonable, but it was something R.J. hadn't given any thought to until now.

"Yeah, he does, but I'm sure Wyatt's talked to him about Valerie's disappearance."

"And Wyatt trusts him?"

Did he? Remembering Wyatt's initial distrust of Jacob, he frowned.

"Jacob helped save Alexis's life," R.J. said thoughtfully, "so yeah, I'd say Wyatt trusts him."

"But you don't. Not entirely."

She was perceptive.

"I don't have any reason to distrust Jacob."

But the truth was, there was something about Jacob that had always put R.J. off. They had nothing in common, and Jacob always seemed a little too glib, his open friendliness somehow insincere.

R.J. felt himself scowling and tried to smooth his features. "Besides, why would Jacob hurt Valerie? He doesn't even know her."

"Are you sure of that?"

The question stopped him. He couldn't be sure. In fact, Jacob wasn't much older than Valerie, now that he thought about it. It was quite possible the two had known each other as kids.

"Did the police search the basement?" Teri demanded.

On firmer ground, R.J. nodded. "They searched the entire house."

"Including that hidden room?"

He had to admire her tenacity. It probably made her a good private investigator, but it was irritating all the same.

"I'm sure they did. Wyatt knows it's here. Kathy and Mrs. Norwhich use that room all the time. It's an open secret. That's why I showed Ian. I didn't want the kid being spooked."

"I think it would take a lot to spook Ian. Although this house is enough to spook anyone."

He had to smile at that. "Yeah, I know. I've lost

some good crew because of this place. Some men refuse to work here."

She didn't smile back. "Word's out that it's haunted, huh?"

His smile faded. "Something like that."

"I'd like to have a look at the basement."

"Why?"

"Call it curiosity."

"Something tells me that satisfying your curiosity is easier said than done."

R.J. sighed when she didn't respond. "All right, but if you think the house is spooky, wait'll you see the basement. I don't know what you expect to find down there. I told you it's empty."

Teri continued to wait in silence.

R.J. shrugged. "All right. I'll see if Kathy will unlock the door for us."

"They keep it locked?"

"Wouldn't you with a kid like Ian in the house?"

Her lips thinned. "R.J., you need to talk to him about sneaking out of bed at night. What if the person he saw wasn't Jacob? He could be hurt."

R.J. ran a hand over his jaw. "Jacob wouldn't hurt a kid."

Her expression expressed her doubt. Belatedly it occurred to him to wonder what Jacob had been doing in the room under the stairs that night. Maybe Wyatt did need to have another talk with Jacob.

"Look, Teri, I don't know the story behind Ian and his mother, but I do know Alexis says he needs to feel he's protecting her. Making his rounds, as he calls it, is a form of security for him. I like Ian."

"I like him, too, but sneaking around the house late at night could be dangerous."

"Heartskeep's spooky, but I'm sure it's safe."

She snorted.

"Despite Valerie's disappearance," he insisted. "Valerie must have left the house for some reason or there would have been signs of a struggle."

"What do you call a broken cell phone?"

"That was outside by the fountain."

"And Ian saw the ghost out there that night."

R.J. jerked. "What?"

"He told me so."

Mentally, he swore. He'd bet Wyatt hadn't bothered talking to the kids about Valerie's disappearance. He never had. And he should have. They both knew Ian liked to walk the house at night.

"What did he see?"

"The blond ghost out by the fountain," she replied in an exasperated tone. "If this Jacob person is supposed to be working in the basement, why was he out by the fountain that night?"

An excellent question. R.J. couldn't think of a single reason.

"Or using this room under the stairs, for that matter?"

"I don't know," he admitted.

The truth was, R.J. didn't know Jacob all that well, even though the younger man spent a great deal of time in and around Stony Ridge. R.J. had shared a beer with him a few times after a softball game, but Jacob didn't play sports. He often came to their games because he was friends with some of the men who did play.

"But you can be sure I'll mention it to Wyatt," he promised.

"Fine, but there's something else you should mention. Lester Boyington and Ian's stepfather are both blonds."

Unease formed a cold, hard ball in the pit of his stomach. "I'll talk to Wyatt," he reaffirmed, "and I'll have a talk with Kathy about Ian."

Teri shook her head. "Ian won't listen to Kathy, but he might listen to you. I got the impression he looks up to you."

R.J. knew that was true. The boy had fastened on him right from the start. He'd gone out of his way to befriend the youngster because he'd seen a lot of himself in Ian at that age. R.J. had been older than Ian when his family perished in a car accident, but he remembered the sense of loss and confusion, the anger, and the need to prove he could control something, anything, in his life. He felt a real empathy for what the boy was going through right now. R.J. would have done anything to protect and preserve part of his own family if he could have.

"I'll talk to him, Teri. And I'll try to make sure Kathy pays attention when he sneaks out of bed from now on. Come on, I'll see about showing you the basement."

Kathy Walsh had stayed at the hospital with Alexis, but Mrs. Norwhich was in the kitchen rolling pie dough on the counter. Teri hung back when R.J. went over to speak with her. R.J. wasn't surprised. Mrs. Norwhich and her dour expression were intimidating to anyone who didn't know her. But R.J. knew there was a warm heart under that gruff exterior and he enjoyed coaxing a smile from her forbidding expression.

"Hey, gorgeous, what are you making?"

Her mouth pinched in automatic disapproval, but her eyes lightened as he slung an arm around her shoulders.

"Pies. And I haven't got any filling ready for you to snitch," she warned sternly.

"I'd settle for a kiss."

She raised the rolling pin warningly, but humor glinted in her pale brown eyes.

"I have work to do, R.J. What mischief are you up to now?"

"Me?" he asked with mock sincerity. "You wound me."

"I will if you touch my pie dough. I have to get these in the oven."

Theatrically, he covered his heart with his hands. "I'm hurt to the core but I'll forgive you if you'll save me a piece of pie. Apple?" he asked hopefully.

"Cherry."

"Yum, that'll do."

Her lips crinkled and she shook her head. "You'd eat anything."

"I would if you made it, but since it isn't ready yet, I was wondering if you'd unlock the basement for me."

"What on earth do you want down there?"

He offered her his best naughty-boy grin and lowered his voice. "You keep pushing me away, so I want to show Teri my etchings."

Mrs. Norwhich glanced to where Teri hovered near the basement door.

"Why didn't you just say the detective wanted to have a look down there?"

"Teri told you she's an investigator?"

Mrs. Norwhich sniffed. "So she claims. If I thought she was any good, I'd put her to work finding my good cutting knife."

A quiver of unease ran through him. "You're missing a knife?"

"Oh, it's probably here someplace. All these helping hands tend to mess up my system."

She put a floured hand in her pants pocket and

withdrew a set of keys, leaving a smear of white in their wake.

"Flashlight's under the sink," she told him with a nod in that direction.

"Aren't the lights working down there?"

"Hmph. There isn't enough light in that basement to see your hand in front of your face," she scoffed. "And mind the mice. They're starting to come inside now that the weather is changing. I don't want them getting in my kitchen."

"Got it. No mice. I'll bring the key right back."

With a curt nod, she returned to her piecrusts. R.J. removed the heavy-duty flashlight from the cupboard under the sink before joining Teri.

"Mice?" she asked.

"Don't tell me you're afraid of a little field mouse?"

"Do you know how many diseases mice carry?"

"No, and I can live without that information, thank you."

She tossed her head. "Don't say I didn't warn you if you catch something fatal."

"You're just full of good cheer, aren't you?"

"Heartskeep brings out the best in me."

"Yeah. It has that effect on lots of people."

And the enormous basement only heightened the effect. Dark as predicted, Teri shuddered as R.J. hit the light switch and twin bare bulbs overhead cast their scanty yellow illumination on the cavernous space.

Ten bulbs wouldn't have brightened all that space. Anything could lurk in a shadow down here and never be seen. There was an eerie chill to the space. Something cold seemed to pass right through her as she took a timid step forward.

"You could hold a football game down here."

"Naw, the ceilings are too low and you'd need more light. Besides, the furnaces would get in the way."

Teri glanced at the two industrial-size furnaces and hot water tanks looming out of the murky sea of emptiness.

"I hate to think what it must cost to heat and air-condition a place the size of Heartskeep."

"A lot," R.J. agreed.

Peering around, she saw strips of what looked like masking tape on the dirty gray floor around the nearest furnace. Other sections of the floor had been marked off, as well. There was even tape running up the walls in two places.

Teri pointed to them. "What's that all about?"

"Will and Jacob are trying to figure out wall positions for the rooms and possible places for a walkout exit." He frowned as he studied the marks.

"Something wrong?"

"No, I'm just thinking what a job it's going to be to excavate, not to mention all the concrete we'll have to dig up to run plumbing and install bathrooms down here. I need to talk to Will. With the size of this job, I need to rethink taking on that Faulkner remodel," he muttered more to himself than her. "Have you seen enough?"

"Yes. There's nothing down here."

"I believe an I-told-you-so is in order."

"Uh-huh, well while you were telling me things, why didn't you mention Corey was taken away?"

She thought she'd managed to control the anger seething inside her, but his startled expression immediately changed to one of contemplation.

"What difference does it make?"

"Where did they take him?"

He searched her face. She did her best to maintain an impassive expression.

"Wyatt placed Corey with a foster couple for the time being," he replied cautiously. "He couldn't stay here with Valerie missing."

"What foster couple?"

Even in the dim light, she could see tension replace his relaxed air.

"Why does it matter?"

"If Valerie is still alive, the first thing she's going to do is go looking for Corey," she snapped.

Obviously, he hadn't thought of that. She could see him running through the possibilities in his head.

"I want to see him," Teri stated quickly.

"Why?"

She let exasperation tinge her voice. "Corey was with Valerie right before she disappeared."

"He's not even two years old! If you were planning to question him, you can forget it. His vocabulary is seriously limited."

She forced her fingers to unclench, but not before he noticed. "I still want to see him."

"Who are you working for, Teri?"

"We've already had this conversation."

"Let's have it again."

She set her jaw. "I can't tell you."

"Can you tell Wyatt? Because I guarantee you're going to have to before he lets you see the boy."

Fear twisted inside her. "He's not going to turn Corey over to Lester, is he?"

"Not until we know more about the situation."

"Like what?" Teri demanded.

"Let's start with where you fit into this picture."

"I told you, I'm here to help them!"

"I know what you told me. What you didn't tell me is why."

"Did you *see* Valerie?" Teri exploded.

"Of course I did."

"And you can ask me that? Isn't that why you brought her here? To help her?"

"So this is personal?"

Teri closed her eyes. He was too good at reading her. "Every job is personal," she told him.

"Then here's something you should know. I spoke to Wyatt before I left the hospital. According to the police in Maryland, the rumor around town is that Valerie is a drug abuser and a manic depressive."

Her eyes flew open. "That's a lie!"

His features clouded. "I don't want to believe it, either, but I don't really know the adult Valerie, and she was nothing but skin and bones and bruises when I saw her."

"Because her husband abuses her!"

"That's what I chose to believe as well, but as Wyatt pointed out, her condition isn't inconsistent with drug abuse, either. And drugs might explain why she disappeared the way she did."

"To get another fix?" Teri sneered. "Some friend you are."

"I didn't say I believe it," he protested, the thread of anger holding her in place, "only that it's what the police are saying."

"So they'll stop looking for her?"

"You know better."

Without another word she turned and hurried back up the stairs. She heard him following more slowly.

His doubts about her seemed to be gaining strength, but there was nothing Teri could do about that. Now more than ever she needed to get to Corey before Lester did.

The police were wrong about Valerie even if Teri couldn't prove it. It may be too late to save Valerie, but Teri *would* save Corey.

Chapter Five

"Teri? Wait."

She stopped as she reached the hall and tried to get her emotions under control before she turned to face him. Like it or not, she needed R.J. But before he could say anything, her cell phone chirped. Knowing who the caller would be, she shook her head at R.J.

"I need to take this," she told him tensely.

Eyes filled with questions, he nodded and walked into the kitchen to replace the flashlight and return the key. Teri hurried down the hall, stopping at the spare bedroom they had used for their earlier conversation.

"Where are you?" Olivia demanded without preamble when Teri answered.

Relief replaced her fear. Her aunt's tone told her she wasn't calling with bad news. Olivia was merely looking for an update.

"A woman's shelter called Heartskeep in upstate New York. Is everything all right?"

"Yes, yes. There's no change. You know what the doctors think."

"They're wrong," Teri said flatly. "She's going to wake up."

Olivia didn't argue. Instead, she changed the subject. "I thought you said they were in Maryland."

Teri sank down on the edge of the bed, suddenly as tired as if she'd had no sleep at all last night. She stared out the window at the side yard without really seeing anything beyond the pattern of rain on the panes of glass.

"They were in Maryland," she told Olivia. "Valerie took off with Corey before I arrived. Three guesses why."

The older woman didn't respond. They both knew exactly why Valerie would have run from her husband.

"I staked out the farmhouse where they were living. When it was obvious no one was there, I went inside."

Olivia inhaled sharply. "Isn't that breaking and entering?"

"Illegal entry," she corrected. "I found an unlocked window. I also found an e-mail to Valerie from a man in Stony Ridge, New York, who offered to get Valerie and Corey into a woman's shelter called Heartskeep."

"Do you think Lester knows where she's gone?"

She pictured Olivia sitting ever so correctly, her stern features strained in concern. "Without a doubt. He found the e-mail before I did, I'm sure of it. Then he showed up as I was leaving."

Olivia gasped. "He caught you there?"

"No. Fortunately, I was able to get away in the fog. I hung around until I was sure he was alone. Then I drove up here to New York."

"He was alone? What does that mean? Do you think he—"

"I don't know what he did or didn't do, but when I got here, I learned that Valerie is missing."

Olivia digested that in heavy silence. There was a quaver in her voice when she finally did speak. "What about Corey?"

Teri closed her eyes for a second, but she couldn't shut out the fear. "The police put him in protective custody."

"Maybe you should go to the police. If you told them who you are—"

"They'd be sure and mention it to Lester when they finally get in touch with him."

"I hadn't considered that. We can't let that horrible man know he didn't succeed in killing you. Can you get Corey away from whoever has him?"

Her resolve hardened. "I'll get him."

Olivia hesitated. "What about the woman?"

"The police think Valerie is some sort of drugged-up head case."

"Dear God. Is she?"

Teri knew her sigh carried across the miles that separated them. "I sincerely doubt it."

"I don't like this."

Teri nearly laughed at the incongruity.

"You will be careful."

There was a small sound at her back. Even before she turned, Teri knew R.J. was standing in the open doorway. What she didn't know was how long he'd been standing there. Quickly she ran through what she'd said to Olivia and decided it didn't matter.

"I have to go," she told the older woman with false calm.

"You'll call me as soon as you find him?"

"You know I will."

"Sorry," R.J. told her as she disconnected. "I didn't mean to interrupt."

"Didn't you?"

She stood to face him as he came all the way into the room.

"I'm not your enemy, Teri."

God, she was tired. "No, you're not."

"But?"

It was absurd, but Teri was suddenly aware of the bed at her side and the fact that the man standing in front of her radiated a calm decisiveness that was far more alluring than his undoubted good looks. She had an inexplicable desire to confide everything in him. For just a moment, she let herself imagine sharing her fears and drawing a measure of comfort from those strong, powerful arms.

No! She couldn't afford to give in to that sort of fantasy. The gentle concern in his eyes could easily mask other, more dangerous emotions. And the absolute last thing she needed was to be sexually attracted to R.J. Monroe. Had she learned nothing?

Teri drew back her shoulders. "Tell me where Corey is."

Suspicion shadowed his gaze. R.J. moved toward her with a lithe, feral grace that momentarily weakened her resolve. She'd been right about one thing, his easygoing manner was a facade. There was more than a hint of the confident predator beneath his friendly smile and warm good looks.

One tension faded as another escalated. His size seemed to dwarf her. Teri forced herself to remain where she stood and ignored the strong impulse to back away.

"Why are you so interested in Corey?" he demanded softly.

Holding his gaze was almost as hard as keeping her voice level. "I told you why."

"Because Valerie will try to get him back? How would she know where to find him? She's more apt to come here."

Before Teri could protest, R.J. continued, "I passed along your concern to Wyatt. He'll see that Corey is protected."

Her heart thudded painfully against the wall of her chest. She could not afford to back down. "If you believe that, you're a fool."

She was the fool. Her brain screamed at her to move away while her body told her something else entirely.

"When it comes to you," he said slowly, "I'm beginning to agree."

She didn't trust him. She didn't want to like him. But when he reached out to run a knuckle along the curve of her jaw, the featherlight touch made her tremble. Her insides clenched expectantly.

She should have been afraid. Why wasn't she afraid?

"What sort of game are you playing, Teri?"

She jerked her head back. The outside edges of panic mingled with the surge of unwanted desire, sending scrambled messages to her brain.

With infinite slowness, he tilted her chin up. He wasn't restraining her in any way. She could step back if she wanted. Why wasn't she moving?

"R.J.?"

The sound of Kathy Walsh calling his name broke the spell that held her in place. R.J. dropped his hand and turned away. Teri jerked away, badly shaken. He'd intended to kiss her.

And she'd been going to let him.

What was wrong with her?

"In here, Kathy."

Kathy came to an abrupt stop in the doorway. Her gaze traveled from one to the other.

"I'm sorry. I didn't mean to interrupt anything."

"You aren't interrupting," R.J. told her smoothly. "Teri and I were discussing where she was going to go from here."

"She's welcome to use one of the empty rooms if she'd like," Kathy offered.

R.J. stiffened. Feeling as though she were coming out of a dream, Teri sidestepped him to put more distance between them and seized the opportunity. "I'd really appreciate that, Kathy."

"I don't think that's a good idea," he objected over her words.

Kathy blinked in obvious confusion.

"For tonight," Teri assured him.

"You can stay at The Inn," R.J. told her with a hard look.

"Valerie didn't disappear from The Inn."

"What difference does that make?"

"If there are clues to what happened to her, they're here at Heartskeep, not at some inn."

His eyes narrowed. "And you think you're going to find these clues?"

His cynical expression hardened her resolve. "It's what I do."

"I'm not letting you upset everyone here," he argued.

"The only one I've upset is you," she countered. "Besides, I've already learned more in a few hours than your police chief did in a day."

"What did you learn?" Kathy asked eagerly.

Teri looked to the older woman with relief. "Ian saw someone out by the fountain the night Valerie disappeared."

"Oh, my." Kathy shot R.J. a pained expression. "I never thought to ask Ian."

"Neither did anyone else," he admitted reluctantly.

"We should have talked to him."

"I know." He turned back to Teri. "But that doesn't mean your staying here is a good idea."

"It beats sleeping in my car or on your couch again."

Their gazes locked. Silently, she dared him to tell Kathy he didn't trust her. R.J.'s scowl deepened. She turned back to the other woman.

"Did Alexis have her baby yet?"

Her worried frown became more animated at the question. "A baby boy, six pounds, nine ounces."

"That's great," R.J. enthused. "Did Wyatt make it there in time?"

"He did, just barely. Everyone is fine. Alexis's sister, Hayley, and her husband, Bram, gave me a lift back to Heartskeep. Looks like their daughter and Leigh and Gavin's daughter will have a new playmate."

R.J.'s smile was genuine. "And so a new Hart dynasty begins."

"True, but I came to find you for another reason," Kathy said. "Mrs. Norwhich needs to get inside the utility closet and the door is stuck shut. Since you're here, do you think you could get it open?"

R.J. swallowed his annoyance with Teri. She had him over a barrel, and she knew it. In order to send her packing, he'd have to admit he'd brought her here under false pretenses. And the truth was, she *had* learned more in a couple of hours than Wyatt and his men had learned in a day of searching. Still, R.J. didn't completely trust Teri and he didn't like the idea of leaving her here at the house with all these vulnerable women. Not that he thought she'd do anything to harm them, it was just…

What? That he was attracted to her and didn't want to be? He thrust the thought aside. His concern was because he didn't know what it was she really wanted. She was keeping her own secrets and that worried him.

"This discussion isn't over," he told Teri.

"Didn't figure it was. I'll get my suitcase, Kathy, if you'll tell me which room to put it in."

"I'll get your suitcase," R.J. stated grimly. "Let me get the door unstuck first."

He strode past Kathy and into the hall, afraid of what he might say if he didn't get his emotions under control. R.J. never lost his temper or his cool, not even on a job site when things went wrong. Teri was the first person in years to slip past that control and tickle his emotions and he didn't like it, not even a little bit.

He'd nearly kissed her a minute ago! What the devil had he been thinking? Okay, he hadn't been thinking, but he'd better start. Teri had a valid point. What if she could find out what had happened to Valerie? Wasn't that the most important issue?

It was almost a relief to turn his frustration on the truculent door. Kathy followed him into the kitchen.

"R.J., is there a reason Teri shouldn't stay here? I thought she was a friend of yours."

Caught, he tried to keep the scowl from his face. "She's more of an acquaintance than a friend," he corrected.

He thought about the gun and crossed mental fingers even as he determined to take it away from her again. He should never have returned it to her in the first place. The last thing Heartskeep needed was a loaded gun with three kids running around at all hours. Ian was too curious for R.J.'s peace of mind.

"And Teri does want Valerie found," he added out loud.

"Why is she so concerned about Valerie? Does she know her?"

"I don't think so." But he suddenly wondered if that was true. She'd never said she didn't know Valerie, and she'd certainly been quick enough to spring to her defense.

"She says she has a client who wants to help Valerie and her son."

"I see," Kathy said faintly. "Should I rescind the invitation?"

Surprisingly, that idea didn't sit any better with him.

"No. It's okay. She really is concerned about Valerie and she's right, she has made some progress here. I'll give Wyatt a call in a little bit and see if he can come out to talk to her."

"I'm not sure you'll be able to pry him away from the hospital any time soon."

"You're probably right, but it will be okay, Kathy."

"All right. If you're sure."

Kathy appeared worried as she moved away and he didn't blame her. He was worried, as well.

AFTER TALKING WITH THEM individually, Teri was convinced that neither young Janet Isley nor Marlene Cosgrove knew anything about Valerie's disappearance, Ian's blond ghost or where Corey had been taken. Betty Drexler was working with the children in the playroom and Teri didn't want to interrupt. It appeared that Evelyn Sutter was lying down, leaving Teri at loose ends. Her goal was to stay out of R.J.'s way until he left and hope he didn't convince Kathy Walsh she should stay elsewhere tonight.

When asked, Marlene had pointed out the corner room near the Sutters' as the bedroom Valerie and

Corey had used. Teri tried the door, only to discover it was locked. Since picking locks wasn't part of her repertoire, she had no choice but to go in search of Kathy to see if she could have a look inside. But as she started toward the back staircase, Evelyn Sutter hailed her from the door of her room.

"Teri? Do you have a moment to speak with me?"

Pleased, Teri joined her. Evelyn's facial bruises were just starting to turn the unbecoming shades of yellow, green and gray that indicated they were on their way to healing. Too bad Teri knew the inner scars wouldn't fade as easily.

"Actually, I was hoping to talk with you, Evelyn, but I didn't want to bother you while you were resting. How are you feeling?"

"I'll be fine, thank you for asking. Would it be all right if we use my room to talk?"

"Sure."

Teri had noted the woman's educated speech patterns earlier. Now she eyed the expensive silk pantsuit Evelyn wore with such careless elegance. Her bearing and the flashy diamond wedding ring glittering on her left hand spoke volumes about her background. Evelyn was obviously used to expensive things and probably a lifestyle very unlike that of the other women here. How was it she had ended up at a battered women's shelter instead of an expensive attorney's office?

The room Evelyn shared with Ian was decorated much like the other bedrooms Teri had seen. The tasteful furniture had been shifted around to allow for cots for children—or, in this case, a single cot—while still leaving a spacious feel to the large room. The depression on the neatly made bed showed that Evelyn had been lying down.

"Have you learned anything about that poor woman's disappearance?" she asked anxiously as soon as she'd closed the bedroom door behind them.

Teri hesitated. Obviously Ian hadn't told his mother about the blond ghost. She suspected he hadn't mentioned the hidden room, either. Based on the little she knew of Ian, she suspected he hadn't wanted to worry his mother.

"I know you probably don't want to discuss the case, but I'm trying to decide if I should take Ian and leave Heartskeep."

Fear, tightly controlled, laced her voice, as well as the gaunt expression on her delicate features. Beneath the swollen eye and facial bruising, Evelyn was lovely in a porcelain-doll sort of way. She was also terribly frightened.

Instinctively, Teri reached for the hand not in a cast. The woman's fingers were cold despite the warmth of the house.

"I understand, Evelyn. Do you have another place to go?"

"No."

The stark word reflected deep-seated pain.

"I haven't spoken with the police yet," Teri told her gently, "so I don't know what they've learned."

The soft, well-cared-for fingers gripped Teri's tightly. "But you did discover something, didn't you?"

Unwilling to lie to her, Teri nodded. "I'm just not sure what it means yet."

"Please, will you tell me? Do you think someone was able to get inside and take her away?"

Teri thought about what she knew. While she wanted to reassure Evelyn, she knew she couldn't provide the sort of assurance the woman was looking for.

"I don't know. I suspect Valerie left the house voluntarily, but I have no evidence either way. What I learned is that a man was seen on the grounds out by the fountain that night."

Evelyn's grip tightened painfully.

"I don't believe he came inside and lured Valerie away. There would have been noise or signs of a struggle if that had been the case. I think, for some reason, Valerie went outside either to get something from her car—possibly her cell phone—or to meet someone."

"You mean a friend?"

Teri hesitated. Valerie would have gone outside to meet R.J. She trusted him, and he did have access to the house and grounds. And though Teri couldn't bring herself to totally trust him, she also couldn't see any reason for R.J. to lure Valerie outside. If he'd wanted to harm her, he could have done so before taking her to Heartskeep.

"I don't know. The cell phone bothers me. It could have fallen from her pocket or something, but I'm thinking she must have been holding it in her hand. That's why the most likely scenario is that she went out to get it from her car."

"And someone grabbed her."

"The man who was seen matches the description of Valerie's husband. I have reason to believe he knew she'd come here."

Evelyn flinched. Teri hurried to offer what little reassurance she could.

"The stranger also matches the description of someone who is known and trusted by the people here. Someone who had the right to be here that night, so he may have nothing at all to do with her disappearance. It's possible that the police chief already knows about this and has ruled out the possibility that he was Valerie's husband."

"But it is also possible that her husband found a way onto the grounds, isn't it?"

Gently, Teri squeezed back and Evelyn released her hand. "I'm not going to lie to you, Evelyn. We both know that's a real possibility. No matter how well a place is defended, a determined person will eventually find a way inside."

With a shudder, Evelyn turned away to stare blindly out the window toward the trees.

"I want to hire you."

For a minute, Teri couldn't process the words. "What?"

Turning desperate eyes back to her, every dignified inch of Evelyn implored her help.

"You're a private investigator. I want to hire you."

Just in time, Teri bit back the automatic rejection. Unconsciously, Evelyn stroked the cast on her injured arm.

"To do what?"

"Protect my son."

The pain of those softly spoken words tore at her heart. "Evelyn—"

"My husband is going to kill me. No one can stop him. I know that. But I'll do anything at all to keep Ian safe."

"The police—"

"I already tried that." She lifted her arm cast. "This is the result. My husband was very angry. He threatened to beat my son if I tried it again. And I know what you're going to say. Yes, I could press charges, but Russell would make bail in less than an hour."

She was right, of course. Men had been sent to prison for abuse, only to kill their victims as soon as they were released. If her husband were determined, nothing would stop him. Teri stared mutely, knowing Evelyn had thought all this through herself.

Evelyn inclined her head. "I see you understand. I'm afraid it took me much longer. You see, I was loved and cosseted my entire life. As an only child, my parents saw to it that I lacked for nothing. I married well the first time. Ian's father was a warm, wonderful man who took up where my parents had left off until a small plane accident ripped my world apart. My husband was a pilot. He was flying my parents to their winter place in Florida in a private plane when it developed engine trouble and went down. There were no survivors."

Teri felt her anguish.

"I was raised to manage a household staff, to host a dinner party for fifty or more, to organize charitable events on a grand scale, but I had never balanced a checkbook or paid a bill in my life. As unbelievable as it may seem to you, I had no idea how to fill out an income tax form or do any of a dozen other mundane chores people take for granted. What I did know how to do was to hire an accountant to help me."

Teri understood better than Evelyn would ever know.

"Russell Eastman was a highly respected, successful CPA and investment counselor when a friend of mine introduced us. Not only did he know how to do all those things, he was charming, well educated and too good to be true. Literally, I'm afraid."

Her eyes clouded at a memory Teri was just as glad she didn't share.

"Sadly, I didn't learn the hidden side of Russell until after we were married and by then it was too late."

"I understand."

"Do you?" Her gaze searched Teri's face. "Perhaps you do. Ian never liked Russell. He saw right through his charm."

"Children often do."

"I wish I'd understood that before I put his life at risk by marrying the man. I thought I was doing the right thing for Ian and me. When I asked Russell to sign a prenuptial agreement, he didn't hesitate."

She closed her eyes against remembered pain. When she opened them once more, Teri was surprised to see a steely determination there. "Will you help us?"

Teri knew her inner turmoil showed. Evelyn regarded her with a steady gaze, and Teri knew she couldn't simply walk away.

"They can't help you here?" she stalled.

"I no longer feel safe here."

No. Heartskeep didn't lend itself to a sense of safety.

"I have to rescue Corey first," she explained, feeling trapped. "And Valerie, if she's still alive."

"I understand, but couldn't you help Ian as well?"

Teri knew she was going to agree even though she had no idea how she was going to accomplish the task.

"I have money—"

Teri shook her head quickly. "Let's not worry about that right now. How did you come to be at Heartskeep?"

"When I fled New York a few days ago, I decided to go to Canada. An old family friend lives there. But after Russell... When the pain got too much for me to drive safely any farther, I stopped at a restaurant and inn outside Stony Ridge. The inn was full for the night, but the clerk was a young woman who was alarmed by my condition. She told me about Heartskeep. Ian was being so brave, but we were both scared and too tired to go any farther. The woman made a call, and Alexis Crossley and her husband arrived a short time later. I didn't know he was a police officer at the time or I probably would have left, but they asked only a few questions and didn't press me for details."

"So there's no way your husband can know this is where you are?"

"I don't see how. I didn't plan to come here, and I waited until he fell asleep that night before I took Ian and fled. I stopped at several ATM machines close to home and took out as much money as I dared. I already had quite a bit of cash on me, so I thought we could manage for a while. I paid cash for my gas and the doctor the Crossleys took me to see. He wanted me to go to the hospital, but I refused. At their urging and my insistence, the doctor agreed to do the exam and set my arm right there in the office. The Crossleys have pull in Stony Ridge," she added with a wry smile.

Teri returned it. "I can imagine."

"I know I wasn't followed here, but sooner or later…"

Yes, sooner or later, her husband would find her.

"I'd say later looks promising," Teri assured her. "It's actually a good thing that you didn't make it to Canada. Your husband will no doubt check with old family friends first. I think you and Ian are safe enough here for right now. Whatever happened to Valerie was directed at her, no one else."

"We still need to disappear."

Teri nodded. It wasn't fair and it wasn't right, it was simply the way things had to be.

"You'll need money and a new identity."

Her face glowed with renewed hope. "Yes."

"We'll have to think about how to do this. Do you have Ian's birth certificate by any chance?"

"Yes. I brought all our important papers with me."

"Good thinking. That will certainly help. I can't make any promises, Evelyn. I'm not a miracle worker. But I will try to help you."

Moisture filled her eyes. "That's all anyone can do. Thank you."

She hugged Evelyn gently and stepped back. "Is there anything you can tell me about Valerie's disappearance? Did you hear her leave her room that night?"

"No. We never really talked. She was only here one day and she kept to herself. We all do, except for Betty and me. Because of the children, you understand. We don't want their schoolwork to suffer unduly."

Teri nodded. In their place, she wouldn't get chummy with strangers, either.

"Do you have any idea where they sent Corey?"

"No, I'm sorry. I was lying down when Chief Crossley arrived. Betty told me a lovely older couple came and spent some time with the little boy. After a very short time, he seemed comfortable with them. Does that help?"

Not nearly enough, but Teri felt a measure of relief. Corey hadn't gone to just anyone, and there was a good chance Betty Drexler knew the couple's name. Once she had that, Teri could find Corey and get him away from here. She'd have to find a way to take Ian and Evelyn as well or come back for them afterward, but she'd worry about that later.

"Thank you for agreeing to protect Ian, Teri."

"Ian's an intelligent boy. I understand your need to protect him, Evelyn, but he needs to know that you intend to protect yourself."

Evelyn blinked in surprise.

"Being cosseted is nice, but standing up for yourself

is far more rewarding. Maybe you don't know how to balance a checkbook. I'm not real great in that department myself. But you're an intelligent, educated woman. You can learn how to do anything you set your mind to doing. Ian's too young to take on the role of your protector. You need to show him that you're prepared to take care of yourself, and him as well."

She couldn't tell what Evelyn was thinking, but for a long moment there was silence.

"In other words, I need to grow a backbone, is that what you're saying?"

"Pretty much. Yes. If you want to survive. I bet if you asked her, Betty could show you how to balance a checkbook."

The anger she expected ghosted across the woman's features, instantly replaced by ironic acknowledgement.

"You don't pull any punches, do you?"

"The truth always hurts, as my aunt likes to say."

"You're absolutely right. It's past time I discovered my backbone."

"It's scary," Teri acknowledged, "but empowering."

"I imagine it is. Thank you again, Teri."

"I haven't done anything yet."

"Yes, you have."

Teri returned her smile. "We'll talk later, all right?"

Evelyn nodded and Teri walked out, closing the door firmly. Somehow, she'd find a way to help the pair, but first, she had to get to Corey before Lester found him.

Chapter Six

R.J. disconnected the call on his cell phone and turned to Mrs. Norwhich. "I don't think this door will give you any more grief now."

"Thank you, R.J. Sounds like you need to be going as well."

"I do. My foreman discovered a problem on a job we've been working on. I need to give him a hand for a few minutes. Do you know where Kathy is?"

"In the library. Someone tracked dirt all over the floor in there."

"Don't look at me. I haven't even been in the library."

Mrs. Norwhich looked meaningfully at Lucky sitting beside him. "I wasn't thinking it was you."

"Hey! It wasn't Lucky, either, unless one of the kids let him out and didn't wipe him down when they let him back in. I'm careful about that."

"I know you are. It was probably one of the children. No harm done either way, just a matter of vacuuming. If you're coming back, I'll save you a piece of pie."

"With that sort of incentive, of course I'll be back."

He gave her a quick hug and headed down the hall, Lucky at his heels. He found Kathy in the library as promised. She turned off the vacuum when he tapped her on the shoulder.

"I have to run over to a job site for a few minutes. Will you let Teri know I'll be back?"

"Of course. Are you sure it's all right for Teri to stay here tonight, R.J.?"

He nodded. "She's legitimately trying to find Valerie, I'm just not sure why. Don't worry about it. I'll be back."

"All right, dear. Try to make it in time for dinner, why don't you? I'm sure Will would enjoy having another male at the table."

"I'll see what I can do, but I can't promise. Come on, Lucky."

After clearing up the problem, R.J. and Lucky swung by the police station to see Wyatt, only to discover the new father had gone back to the hospital to visit his wife and son. R.J. was nearly at Heartskeep when he decided to head to his place first and change clothes. It meant he'd miss dinner, but he was already going to be late and Mrs. Norwhich's leftovers would be just as good reheated. Besides, Lucky needed something to eat, as well, and Heartskeep didn't stock dog food.

After feeding Lucky, he'd see how Teri was getting along with everyone. At least, that was what he tried to tell himself. The truth was, it was an excuse to see her again and he knew it.

He didn't trust her, wasn't even sure he liked her, but he couldn't stop thinking about the aggravating woman. Who was she working for? What was she hiding? And why did he keep wondering what it would be like to kiss her?

His headlights picked up a pond of water at the bottom of his street, bringing him to a halt. Not good. At this rate, the street would be impassable soon. As it was, he wouldn't have driven through the water in anything smaller than his heavy truck. Even that was taking a chance. The police needed to close Stony Creek Road and the cross street leading to the highway. Of course, that would mean going miles around to get onto the highway.

"Come on, Lucky, let's make this fast. We're going to spend the night at Heartskeep if they'll let us. Otherwise we could be trapped here come morning." Which was one of the not-so-good perks to living this far out.

Lucky sat up on the seat attentively, peering straight ahead into the utter darkness that surrounded them. As soon as R.J. started up his drive, he knew he was really pressing his luck. The ruts were a quagmire and the truck was in danger of bogging down.

"First thing tomorrow, I'm ordering a load of fresh gravel, Lucky. What good is running my own crew if I don't use them when I need them? Come on, fella. We're going to grab your food and feed you at Heartskeep."

Water sucked at his heavy work boots as he trudged to the back door. Lucky paused briefly to lift his leg, but was right there as soon as the door was unlocked. He didn't seem to like the windblown rain in his face any more than R.J. did.

The generator was still running, but he needed to add some fuel to it before he left. He quickly gathered items together and shoved them into a duffel bag. Lucky waited impatiently by the mudroom door.

"You were just out there."

Lucky barked without looking away from the door.

"All right, but make it fast."

Lucky growled low in his throat as he plunged outside. R.J. froze. Lucky rarely growled and never for no reason, as he'd learned the other night. For all his size, Lucky didn't have a vicious bone in his body.

R.J. tried calling him back. As expected, the dog ignored him. Once he was on the scent of something, he wouldn't pay any attention until he was good and ready.

As R.J. carried his bag out to the truck, a burst of gunshots was followed by a yelp of pain that could only have come from Lucky. Tossing his duffel bag inside, he took off running, reaching for his cell phone to press 911.

Someone plunged through the woods running for the road. Part of his brain noted the bark of the tree beside him splintering as another volley of shots was fired. This time, the person was shooting at him! Despite that, R.J. continued moving forward, the sound of Lucky's whimpers drawing him on.

"This is R.J. Monroe out at the old Teller place," he told the emergency dispatcher. "Someone just shot my dog and took several shots at me. He's running for Stony Creek Road."

R.J. nearly stumbled over Lucky before he saw him. The dog was crawling toward him, whining pitifully.

"Easy boy. Take it easy." A long tongue came out to lick his hand gratefully.

"Tell Wyatt I'm taking Lucky to Doc Handleman's place," he continued to the dispatcher.

Without listening to the response, he disconnected. Lucky yelped in pain as R.J. lifted the heavy animal and hurried back to his truck. The overhead light revealed blood matting Lucky's fur.

"It's okay, boy. It's going to be okay."

It had to be okay. The tightness in his chest was so intense R.J. could hardly breathe. He would have torn down the drive if he hadn't been afraid to jar the wound too much. Lucky lay still, whimpering softly as though he understood R.J. was doing his best to get help.

Taillights were disappearing around the curve in the road when he reached the end of his driveway. He couldn't tell the make, but he thought the vehicle was a light-colored sedan. He cursed, wishing he could give chase.

Water at the bottom of the hill splashed against the truck's frame as he went through the gathering stream. Too bad the bastard who had shot Lucky hadn't taken this route. A small car would never have made it through. In another few minutes, he wouldn't have made it, either.

R.J. pushed the truck for all the speed he could man-age given the road conditions, while fumbling for his cell phone once more. Since Doc played softball with him, he had the number on speed-dial. Doc's wife an-swered on the second ring.

"Marion, it's R.J. Some bastard just shot Lucky. I'm on my way in with him. He's bleeding bad."

"I'll tell Lou. We'll meet you at the clinic door, R.J."

"Thanks."

He called the dispatcher back and let her know the direction the shooter had taken. The woman promised to pass the information on to Wyatt. Disconnecting, he laid his hand on the large dog's head and gave the truck more gas.

IAN WAS GLAD Nola and Boone weren't around to see how nervous he was. When he'd sneaked downstairs, it had barely been raining. Now a thunderstorm raged overhead. Loud noises tended to remind Ian of *him* when he was in a rage.

Thunder echoed the streak of lightning that brightened the room despite the drapes he'd pulled across the library windows. Ian huddled deeper into the wing chair, the book slipping from his fingers mostly forgotten. The lights flickered once more but stayed on. He reached for the flashlight he'd set on the small round table, nearly knocking over the lamp.

Shadows curled around the edges of the room, looming menacingly with each display from the heavens. The storm hadn't been this bad when he'd slipped in here shortly after his mother had left the bedroom, thinking him safely in bed for the night. Something was troubling her and not just the storm. He wished she'd talk to him. Instead, she had that sad look in her eyes that made him feel so bad inside he couldn't stand it.

A really loud crash of thunder made him jump. Maybe tonight hadn't been such a good night to read about ghosts. He'd better put the book back and go upstairs before his mom decided to go to bed for the night. He'd known it was a risk coming down here this early, but he'd wanted to check out the book on poltergeists Nola had mentioned. Unfortunately, there were so many books in the library that he'd wasted a lot of time searching before he'd found it.

A tree branch scraped the window beside the fireplace, leaving eerie fingers of wood shadowed against the drape in a brilliant flash of light that split the night. Thunder crashed almost at the same time. Ian yelped out loud. The light went out, plunging the room into total darkness.

His hand shook so hard he could barely turn on his flashlight. The batteries were dying, and the weakened beam hardly lit anything. He could hear his breathing coming in fast pants as if he'd been running. Running was what he wanted to do, but there were still people awake all over the house. He'd heard Mrs. Walsh talking to Mr. Leftcowitz when he'd come down the stairs.

Mr. Leftcowitz was pretty nice. He talked kind of quiet and right at you, even if you were just a kid, but Ian couldn't let anyone know he was down here. He'd have to sneak back upstairs without being seen. He shivered with cold and a trace of fear. Holding the book he could no longer see to replace, he crept to the door. Lightning and thunder continued their assault. Wind drove gusts of rain against the windows as if it were trying to shove its way past the glass.

Edging the door open a crack, he stopped. There were voices in the hall. Mr. Leftcowitz, Mrs. Walsh and Teri stood near the front door talking. Ian would have to leave through the office next door so they wouldn't see him.

The flashlight's beam was enough to show him the path between the twin couches. He skirted them and darted into the office. In this room, the storm's fury was all too visible because the drapes hadn't been pulled. Trees danced and swayed outside, highlighted by the ugly slashes of light that forked the sky.

Ian tried not to look toward the windows. He ran to the door that gave onto the hall. Easing it open, he paused to listen.

A scraping noise came from the library at his back. Fear climbed his throat, riveting him in place. There couldn't be anyone in there. He would have heard if someone had opened the door from the hall.

Unless it was the ghost.

Curiosity proved stronger than his fear. It drew him back toward the opening between the two rooms. Next to the fireplace, a shadow detached itself from the other shadows and began to move briskly across the floor. A flash of lightning was all it took to reveal the familiar shape of the blond ghost.

The heavy book slipped from his fingers. No longer caring if he was seen, Ian fled, expecting to feel ghostly fingers on his neck at any moment as he raced into the hall and ran for the back stairs and the safety of his room.

LOU AND MARION HANDLEMAN operated their veterinary practice out of their home, a sprawling old farmstead where Marion raised horses. Wyatt pulled into the driveway right behind R.J., lights flashing. Doc came outside to help carry the wounded dog while Marion held the door.

"Seems to be the night for emergencies. The Brunnels just left. Their Lab got the worst of a fight with the Jensen's German shepherd. You'll probably be hearing from them, Wyatt. They were not happy with the Jensens. How ya doin' Lucky? Don't you know to stay away from men with guns? Let's get him on the table and I'll have a look."

Marion quickly shooed R.J. and Wyatt out of the room. RJ then told Wyatt what little he knew.

"Could be someone was lost, came asking for directions and was scared when Lucky charged him," Wyatt suggested.

"Someone who just happened to come armed and then took a couple of shots at me?"

"Yeah, I don't buy it, either. You have any irate customers recently?"

R.J. scowled. "No, but if Teri's right, maybe an irate husband."

"That private investigator you told me about?"

"Yeah. She claims Boyington is dangerous. Based on what he did to Valerie…"

"What you assume he did to Valerie."

"…I'd say he's the most likely culprit."

"Let me make a few calls." Wyatt pulled out his cell phone. R.J. paced the waiting room to give him privacy. Long minutes later, Wyatt came over and laid a hand on his shoulder.

"Boyington drives a black BMW," he told R.J., "with Maryland plates."

"I didn't see the plates, but I'm pretty sure this car was light-colored. It could have been a rental."

"Possibly. We'll check it out."

The door opened and Doc came up to them. "That dog of yours really lives up to his name," he told R.J. He handed Wyatt a vial with a piece of metal inside. "This bounced off his ribs, missed everything vital and landed in some soft tissue. The second shot grazed his back right above this one. He's going to be fine, but I'll have to keep him overnight."

"Can I see him?"

"Sure, but he's pretty heavily sedated. Go on back, Marion's just cleaning up."

When R.J. returned, Wyatt was waiting for him.

"I spoke with Chief Hepplewhite in Fools Point. They still haven't been able to reach Boyington, but the police chief told me something interesting. The farm next to the Boyingtons' is run by a couple who have a son around Valerie's age. He lives and works in Frederick, not far from them. Seems he disappeared a few days before Valerie Boyington."

"Does the chief think there's a connection?"

Wyatt sighed. "We don't know. His parents are the last people known to have seen their son alive and they're pretty distraught. They do say he'd met Valerie."

"You're thinking she ran off with him."

"I'm not thinking anything, yet. I'm just relaying the information we have right now. This man had a couple of arrests for possession of marijuana and drug paraphernalia a few years ago, but the parents believe he'd finally gotten his life on track. Hepplewhite knows the young man personally and says he's known to have a temper."

"And you think maybe he's responsible for Valerie's condition?"

"Like I said, I'm making no assumptions at this point, R.J. Realistically, we have to look at the possibility that this man's disappearance and Valerie are connected somehow."

"And the drugs?"

"His parents swear he doesn't do them anymore. His employer does random drug testing and he's never failed a test yet. But it's possible he still had connections. Maybe he hooked Valerie up with the wrong people."

R.J. shook his head. "I don't buy it, Wyatt. I don't think Valerie was doing drugs."

"That's friendship talking. The fact is, you don't know Valerie well enough to know what she was or wasn't involved in. We need to consider everything. There's no sign of foul play at the young man's apartment or anywhere else. All Chief Hepplewhite knows is that he didn't show up for work one morning and he and his car are missing."

R.J. swore softly. He wanted to refute Wyatt's words, but knew he couldn't.

"Hepplewhite seems like a good cop. He's looking into all this from his end, including running a check to see if there's a gun registered to the young man, his parents or either of the Boyingtons. Maybe we can match this shell if so. In the meantime, I think you should spend the night at my place. They aren't releasing Alexis and the baby until morning, so I'm baching it anyhow."

"I didn't even think to ask how they are doing."

"You've had a few other things to think about, but they're fine. Wonderful, in fact. We're going to name him Jameson Brian Crossley after our fathers."

"I like it."

"Yeah."

They shared a grin before R.J. shook his head. "I appreciate the offer, Wy, but I was thinking I'd see if I could crash at Heartskeep tonight. Kathy offered Teri a room for the night."

Wyatt raised his eyebrows in question.

"It isn't that I don't trust her, but I don't know who she's working for and I thought given everything that's happened—"

"Where is Teri licensed?"

"I didn't think to ask. Her car has Texas plates."

Wyatt frowned as his two-way radio began squawking in his ear. After a terse conversation, he told R.J. he had to leave.

"We have four idiots trapped in Stony Creek. The highway exit and the road to your place are flooded out."

"Go."

"I'll call you later. If you change your mind—"

"I'll go to George and Emily's."

Wyatt looked as if he wanted to say something else, but his radio started up again. R.J. went back to see Lucky one more time, paid Doc and headed for his car. It had almost stopped raining, but the temperature was falling swiftly. Wyatt was going to have his hands full tonight.

R.J. called Kathy and filled her in. As he expected, she immediately invited him to spend the night at Heartskeep. Before he even reached the driveway of the old mansion, it began to storm again, shooting lightning across the sky.

Teri and Kathy were waiting at the front door when he hurried onto the porch. The house was completely dark.

"Get in here before you get electrocuted."

"How's Lucky?" Teri demanded at the same time.

"Recovering. Did you lose the electricity?"

Kathy nodded. "Will went out back to start the generator."

R.J. was relieved he didn't have to do it. The events of the night were starting to take their toll, and he was suddenly very tired.

"Thanks for putting me up tonight, Kathy. They've closed the road near the highway entrance."

"I'm not surprised. Will's talking about starting on an ark if this keeps up."

"Not a bad idea."

"Have you eaten?"

"No, but I'm not hungry." Though he'd skipped dinner, it was true. The house lights came to life, making them all blink.

"You have blood all over your coat," Kathy told him. "Let me have it and I'll sponge off what I can. You can

put your bags in the spare room nearest the kitchen. You
need to eat something. I'll warm you up a plate."

Taking his coat, Kathy hurried away before he could
protest, leaving him staring into Teri's worried expression.

"What happened, R.J.?"

Her genuine concern touched him. On the way down
the hall to drop off his bag, he told Teri about the evening. Then he had to repeat it all for Will and Kathy as
Kathy set a heaping plate in front of him. To his surprise, he finished every bite, including the slice of
warmed cherry pie with ice cream.

"Seems to me you three have quite a mystery on
your hands," Will said.

"Three?" R.J. asked.

"You, Teri and Wyatt. Did you ever think maybe it
was Valerie who shot at you?"

"No," Teri and R.J. said as one. Their gazes met and
held.

"I don't believe it," R.J. finished.

"Me, either," she agreed. "It was Boyington."

"Could she have been seeing this neighbor?" R.J.
asked.

Teri hesitated. "I don't know," she said after a moment. "We don't have enough information."

"Well, you aren't going to solve anything tonight,"
Kathy told them. "And you look done in, R.J. You, too,
Teri. I think we could all use a good night's sleep."

"Are you staying over?" R.J. asked Will.

"Might. I was supposed to meet Jacob tonight, but
I doubt he's going to show, given the weather."

"He'd have to drive all the way into Stony Ridge and
double back to get here," R.J. agreed. "And they might
have closed the town exit, as well. That area tends to
flood, too."

Teri shuddered.

Kathy picked up the dirty dishes over R.J.'s protest. "You three can do what you like, but I'm arming the security system and heading for bed. I have to be up early tomorrow."

They all turned to the bank of windows as lightning splintered the sky in an incredible display.

"Use the room next to R.J.'s," Kathy told Will. "You can't go out in that."

"I think I will," he agreed.

In minutes the kitchen emptied, leaving Teri and R.J. alone.

"I'm glad Lucky's going to be all right."

R.J. nodded. "Me, too."

"I guess I'll go on up to bed myself. There really isn't anything else we can do tonight."

"No."

Neither of them moved. She was standing close enough that R.J. could smell the light fragrance he was coming to associate with her. Not really a perfume. Scented soap, or maybe shampoo. He couldn't decide, but he liked it.

"Well, I guess I'll go upstairs."

"Teri?"

"What?"

He reached for her slowly, giving her plenty of time to pull away. Instead, she stared up at him from behind thick, curling black lashes. Her vivid eyes mirrored the strong desire suddenly rushing to fill him with need. He discovered her lips were even softer than the silken strands of her hair beneath his fingers.

R.J. meant to keep the kiss simple. At least, that's what he told himself. But as soon as she moved into his arms, fitting herself against him as though she'd been made just for him, he knew it for a lie. He wanted her with a fierce intensity that shocked him to the core.

R.J. liked women. He enjoyed their company and all the differences that made them so intriguing. But he'd never before felt this irrational urge to possess a woman so completely.

When her lips parted, he deepened the kiss and his erection pressed against her in taut demand. Her body stilled. Her eyes flashed open. He saw the first stirrings of nerves there. Instantly, he let her go and stepped back.

"Sorry." And he was. The force of his hunger for her shook him. He stared at her brightly flushed cheeks and the soft, just-kissed look of her quivering lips. "That got out of hand."

"Yes."

"Are you all right?"

Her eyes gleamed brightly. "It was just a kiss."

"Fine. It was just a kiss. What would you say to a brief affair?"

She lowered her lashes, hiding her initial response before regarding him with an outwardly calm expression.

"I'd say no. I'll be leaving tomorrow."

He didn't want her to leave. Not yet. Not until he understood her. Or at least understood why he was so fascinated by her.

"As soon as I talk to Betty Drexler and check out the room Valerie used while she was here, I'll be on my way. If you won't take me to see Corey, there isn't much else I can do."

That centered his thoughts. "Why are you so determined to see her son?"

"Part of my job is to find the two of them. Since Valerie had a child with her, I need to make sure that child is Corey Boyington."

The suggestion that it might be another child stunned him.

"Who else could it be?"

"I won't know until I see him, will I?"

"Hold it. Why would you even think such a thing? What's really going on here, Teri? Why won't you tell me who hired you?"

"Confidentiality is everything in my line of work. I'd need permission first."

"Get it."

"Why? Because you said so? You really do think highly of yourself, don't you?"

"Yes, but the point is, maybe I could be of more help if I understood what your role is really all about."

He saw the automatic brush-off coming and held up a hand to forestall her.

"Look, Valerie is the sister of one of the best friends I ever had. Finding her is important to me, too."

"So the two of you did have something going?"

The suggestion that it might have been jealousy in her tone held his annoyance at bay.

"Valerie and Eric's family were wealthy," he told her after a moment's silence. "None of them cared that I was the foster kid with the temper and a history of getting into trouble. That may not mean anything to you, but it meant a great deal to me, then and now. Eric talked me out of going to a party one night with a couple of guys I knew. He invited me to his place instead."

He managed a shrug, but he couldn't dismiss the memory. He'd been an angry teen back then, with very few expectations and even fewer friends. Yet while Eric had money and wealthy friends, he'd never made R.J. feel inferior.

"That party turned into a drunken brawl. Someone pulled a knife and a kid we knew ended up in the hospital. I was identified as being part of the group. One person even I said I was the one who'd had the knife. Eric's entire family showed up at the police station to shoot that down. After that, they made a place for me in their home. I was always welcome as Eric's friend. He got me involved in sports. We were always trying to outdo one another."

R.J. smiled at the memory. He wished Eric could see how his life had finally worked out. He realized Teri was watching him intently as she measured the sincerity of his words, but there was no sign of pity in her expression.

"Valerie hero-worshipped her brother and, yes, she had a crush on me, but she was just a kid."

"She's not a kid now."

"No, she's the sister of my best friend. That means something to me. If I can do anything at all to help Eric's sister, I will."

Her expression softened. "I believe you. I'll talk to my client in the morning," she promised finally.

"Fair enough."

"We'd both better get some sleep."

"Want me to walk you to your room?"

"I know the way."

"Well, darn."

The smile hit her eyes first. "Good night, R.J."

"'Night."

His gaze followed her as she made her way to the back stairs. She didn't turn around.

She wasn't beautiful, and she had enough distrust for

ten women. That sharp tongue of hers could flay a man alive—or bring him incredible pleasure. She wasn't even his type.

But he still wanted her.

Chapter Seven

Teri lay perfectly still. She didn't know what had pulled her from sleep, but she was ice-cold and the dry taste of fear filled her throat. Her heart beat an erratic tattoo.

She listened hard, straining for any sound. There was none in the dark room, but she knew there had been. Her eyes flashed to the travel alarm she'd placed on the nightstand. One-fifteen. She'd been asleep for more than an hour, despite the scene in the kitchen.

R.J. had kissed her and she'd kissed him back. And no matter what she'd told him afterward, if he hadn't moved so fast...

What? She would have made love with him?

Of course not. Yet, she could still feel his mouth on hers, the hardness of his body and the yearning desire that had been hers as well as his. And he'd backed off. The moment he sensed she was uncomfortable, he had stopped.

But she had to focus on the present. Someone had been in her room. She knew it with the certainty of the hunted.

There was still no sound. She couldn't just lie there like some helpless animal.

Teri rolled from the bed, reaching for the flashlight

beside the alarm clock at the same time. She swept the beam over her room. Empty.

Her fingers shook as she turned on the table lamp, flooding the room with a soft yellow light. Still empty. Nothing appeared disturbed except…had that closet door been partly open before? Maybe. She couldn't remember.

Teri reached under the mattress and withdrew the loaded gun she'd placed there for safekeeping. The heavy, ugly metal gave her a measure of security, but it didn't stop her from trembling.

"Come on out. I've got a gun and I'm not afraid to use it."

Silence, utter and complete.

Feeling only slightly foolish, she moved toward the door until she could edge it open all the way with her foot. The gun wavered in her hand as shivers raced up and down her arms. The closet was empty.

Teri moved to the connecting bathroom. That door was still locked. So was the door to the hall. Still, something had pulled her from sleep, and the sense that her space had been violated remained.

Reluctantly she turned off the light and picked up her flashlight. Tucking the gun into the pocket of the sweatpants she'd slept in, she moved to the hall door and turned the lock slowly so it wouldn't make any noise.

The house sat in eerie silence. Nothing moved. She crossed to the three steps that led down to the balcony railing before she lost her nerve. In the dining room below, a small flash of light came and went so quickly she almost thought she'd imagined it. She held her breath and waited.

Lightning?

Her gaze flicked to the skylights overhead. No sign of lightning, only the impenetrable blackness of the night. A flashlight, then.

Teri's hand started for her gun and stopped. She'd watched Kathy set the house alarm. Maybe it wasn't an intruder. Maybe R.J. was checking—

No, of course, Ian making his rounds.

She'd have to make sure, but she was willing to bet on it. Except what had woken her? She strove to remember, convinced it had been a sound. Ian brushing against her door? Maybe he had tried the knob.

Possible.

Or maybe R.J. had come upstairs. The thought shouldn't send that strange thrill shooting through her. She did not want to get involved with R.J. Okay, she wanted it, but she couldn't and that was all there was to that.

The decision helped her start for the staircase. R.J. needed to talk to Ian. The boy could get hurt prowling around like this. What if he'd come inside her room? She might have shot him!

Teri paused. The gun was an uncomfortable weight in her pocket. She didn't like guns. They were a last resort, a desperate measure to stay safe. She didn't need to walk around with a gun here in Heartskeep. A good strong yell would bring all sorts of people running.

Like R.J.

Nervously, she returned to her room and shoved the gun back under the mattress. Then she hurried to the stairs. If it wasn't R.J. moving around down there, she'd wake him and he could go with her to confront Ian. Ian would listen to R.J.

Running lightly across the cold kitchen floor, she hurried to the hall and R.J.'s room, wishing she'd taken time to put on some shoes. The door to his room was closed. Thankfully, she discovered it wasn't locked.

R.J. was curled on his side, breathing so peacefully she hated to disturb him. His features were even more handsome in repose with those long, curling lashes resting like midnight against his cheekbones. His tousled hair and trouble-free expression took years from his age, making him seem less hard and dangerous. One bare arm and shoulder were exposed, revealing the lean healthy muscles she had glimpsed before through the rain-slicked windows of his living room.

She hoped he didn't sleep nude. But the thought caused a thrilling tingle low in her belly.

"R.J.? R.J., wake up."

He didn't stir.

"R.J.?" She laid her hand on the warm, bare skin of his forearm.

He came awake in a sudden burst of motion. Before she could take a step back, a steely grip took her arm, knocking the flashlight from her hand. He sat up and the covers dropped from the planes of his bare chest.

"R.J. it's me—Teri!"

"Teri? What the hell?"

He released her, and she jumped back.

"I'm sorry. Did I hurt you? What's wrong? What are you doing here? What time is it?"

"There's someone moving around in the house," she managed.

"What? Where?"

Tossing aside the covers, he came off the bed in an almost feline spring that had her stepping back against the window. The flashlight rolled to the middle of the bed and pointed right at him. Its beam revealed a pair of dark briefs covering the area where her gaze was instantly drawn. Very brief briefs.

She tore her gaze from the sight of the flat planes of his abdomen and the line of dark hair that arrowed down to disappear behind the slim band of cloth.

"There's someone moving around down here. It's probably Ian." She hated the tremor in her voice that made her sound weak and frightened, but he didn't seem to notice.

"Where?"

The demand steadied her. "I saw the flash of light in the dining room. I think it was heading toward the living room."

"Wait here."

"Aren't you going to put your pants on?"

He gave her an exasperated look. "No."

He was already moving for the door. Teri hesitated, then snatched up her flashlight and hurried after him.

BY THE TIME Ian was satisfied that the ground floor appeared secure, he needed to use the bathroom. He slipped into the one between the office and the library and set his flashlight on the counter. Though he was fairly sure no one was awake at this hour, there was no point in advertising his presence so he didn't bother turning on the light.

He'd checked everything except the library. He was saving that room for last. He'd had plenty of time to think about things since he'd run upstairs like a scared rabbit several hours ago. It seemed to him that there were two possibilities. Either a real ghost had appeared in there right after he left the room, or the fireplace in the library was like the one in the dining room and hid yet another secret room. He liked that idea best, except it meant the figure hadn't been a ghost after all.

The idea that it had been a man really worried him because he knew it hadn't been Will. He should have yelled. Terri, Mr. Leftcowitz and Mrs. Walsh would have come running. They would have caught the intruder.

He'd thought about this for hours after he'd gone back upstairs. He had almost gone looking for R.J. and Teri to tell them what had happened. Except his mother had come upstairs to get ready for bed and he had to pretend he was asleep.

Maybe R.J. knew about this fireplace. Maybe he knew about the man, too. He might even be angry that Ian had seen the stranger. Ian didn't want to take that chance.

As he flushed the toilet there came a muffled groaning, clanking sound unlike any noise he had ever heard before. It wasn't coming from the toilet. It seemed to come from the tile walls of the bathroom itself.

Paralyzed, Ian stood rooted to the spot listening. The sound stopped as abruptly as it had begun. Then he heard a faint, low moan and a ghostly, echoing voice. A masculine voice. An angry voice.

Or an angry ghost.

Terror sent him fleeing for the hall. Ian was no longer certain that ghosts could not harm humans.

R.J. WAS HALFWAY DOWN THE HALL when the bathroom door off the office opened and a small figure erupted, barreling straight at him.

"Ian?"

The beam from Teri's flashlight froze the child midflight. Fear left him staring at them wide-eyed. R.J. hurried forward. Something was very wrong.

"What is it, Ian? What's wrong?"

"R.J.?" The boy was shaking badly. "The ghost. In the bathroom."

"Get him back to the room," R.J. ordered as Teri reached their side. He snatched the flashlight from her unresisting fingers and sprinted for the bathroom. The door was ajar. R.J. kicked it open the rest of the way. The spacious room was empty, but R.J. knew a second door led into the office. Flinging that open, he stepped inside.

The room appeared empty, but that didn't mean anything. The house was a blasted maze. By now, an intruder could have gone through the library and be out in the hall. From there, he could cross to the left wing and be anywhere in a matter of seconds.

R.J. swore under his breath and returned to the main hall. Teri and Ian stood exactly where he'd left them. With a mental curse he bore down on them, his anger born of fear.

"I told you to get him back to my room."

"It wasn't what he saw, it was what he heard," Teri snapped at him.

"What are you talking about?"

"The ghost was moaning and rattling chains," Ian chimed in. Fear lingered in his voice and expression, but he was pulling it together. "I heard him in the wall of the bathroom."

R.J. bit back another oath. "Show me."

Ian led the way. The finger that pointed at the wall butting against the library quivered.

"It came from there."

The boy's fear had quickly changed to excitement now that he had backup. While R.J. wanted to dismiss his tale, he knew Ian had heard something. He began running his fingers along the cool tiles, trying to visualize what stood on the other side of this wall.

"What are you doing?" Teri asked.

"Looking for a hidden entrance."

"In a bathroom?"

"I think there's one in the library," Ian said excitedly. "The ghost appeared in there earlier tonight."

"What are you talking about?" R.J. demanded.

Ian looked nervously from him to Teri. She immediately laid a reassuring hand on his shoulder.

"Stop scaring him," she ordered protectively.

The question *had* come out sounding harsher than he'd intended, but Teri's indignant response was irritating.

"I'm not trying to scare him. I'm trying to figure out what's going on here."

"Well you aren't going to get any answers by snarling at him," she snapped.

"I am *not* snarling!"

She met his glare with one of her own. "Your fangs are showing."

He took a step toward her.

"Don't hit her!" Ian cried as he jumped between them.

R.J.'s gut twisted at the fearful resolve on the boy's face. Instantly contrite, he dropped to one knee in front of Ian.

"I'd never do that, Ian. Never."

Ian looked uncertain. His lower lip quivered, but there was fierce determination in his drawn features. R.J. met Teri's stricken gaze.

"While it might be tempting to wring her lovely neck at times, I would never strike a woman in anger, Ian."

"You're mad at her."

"No he's not, Ian," Teri interjected. "He's frustrated

so he's snapping at me like a bear with a sore paw, but he'll get over it. R.J. wouldn't hurt me."

His gut took another punch at her immediate and obviously sincere defense of him. R.J. ran a hand over his jaw. He could feel the scrape of morning bristles beginning to show. Ian stared from one to the other, obviously unconvinced.

R.J. stood, more touched than he wanted to admit by Teri's faith in him.

"She's right, Ian. I tend to be grumpy when I'm awakened from a deep sleep. But I would never hurt a woman, no matter how much she irritates me."

She planted her hands on her hips. "Right. Blame it on the woman," she said with exaggerated annoyance.

The corners of his mouth lifted. To Ian, he added, "See how it is? If I tried anything with Teri, she'd deck me. She probably knows karate or something."

"Bank on it."

"You aren't scared?" Ian asked her.

"Of R.J.? No way. He's all bark, no bite."

He promised retaliation with a glance at her before turning to the puzzled boy.

"Despite what you saw between your mother and your stepfather, Ian, men and women can argue without resorting to violence."

"But you looked so mad."

"Frustrated," Teri corrected.

"And tired," he added. "I was sound asleep until she woke me a few minutes ago."

"Grumpy."

"What we'd better do is have a quick look at that library so we can all get back to bed before we have to get up again."

"That's what I was going to do until I heard the

ghost start making all that noise. Is there another hidden room by the fireplace in the library?"

Ian looked at him hopefully.

"No, not that I know of. Why?"

"Then it really was a ghost."

"What was?" Teri asked.

"I was in there earlier when you were in the hall talking to Mrs. Walsh and Mr. Leftcowitz. I was just getting a book," he added hurriedly, "but I didn't want my mom to know I was out of bed so I started to cut through the office. The ghost appeared in the library as soon as I left."

"You saw him?"

Ian nodded at R.J. who looked to Teri for confirmation. She shrugged.

"It must have been when we were waiting for you. No one came out of there while we were in the hall."

Tension ran through him. "I guess none of us are going to sleep until we check it out."

"Come on," Ian urged, starting down the hall.

"Don't you think you should put some pants on first?" Teri cautioned. "You don't want to be shocking the residents."

R.J. scowled, but she was right. "Wait here. I'll be right back."

"What do you think?" Teri whispered as they followed Ian down the hall a few minutes later.

"I think I'm really starting to hate Heartskeep."

"Me, too," she agreed.

Despite the lights R.J. flipped on, the edges of the library remained shrouded in shadows as they made their way to the fireplace and the bookcases that surrounded it.

"It'll go faster if you take one side and we take the other," Teri suggested.

"Fine, just don't get your hopes up. This is an outside wall. I don't remember any jogs in the building that would indicate a hidden room—"

He swallowed an oath as the bookcase Ian had been examining on his left suddenly moved back with a scraping sound. A narrow, dark opening was revealed.

"Cool!" Ian exclaimed.

R.J.'s stomach knotted. He shared a worried look with Teri. From past experience, R.J. knew that trouble usually followed the discovery of hidden rooms at Heartskeep.

"Not good," he muttered.

"You're expecting an argument? It's not very wide."

"And it's dark," Ian agreed in a hushed tone.

R.J. stepped between them to throw the beam of the flashlight into the narrow space. It wasn't deep or long. Pine needles, mud, dirt and what appeared to be a dirty rag littered the unfinished floor. Poking at the rag cautiously, he realized it was exactly what it seemed. Someone had used the rag to wipe at damp, wet feet. He remembered Kathy running the vacuum in the library, muttering about someone making a mess.

"There's only enough space for a person to stand," Teri said at his back. "It doesn't go anywhere. Why would anyone build a place to just stand?"

Pine needles crunched as he stepped inside. "They wouldn't."

His fingers ran down the wood looking for a release mechanism. He found the catch and a section of the outside wall slid open behind a large yew.

Teri made a small noise of surprise. Ian offered up another "Cool!" as R.J. squeezed outside behind the overplanted yews growing against the house. Wet branches slapped at him. He was glad now that he'd taken the time to throw on a shirt and pants. Despite the clothing, a cold damp breeze raised goose bumps along his flesh. He consoled himself with the thought that at least it wasn't raining any longer.

A large pine tree stood a few feet away. The thick branches would block a person's view of this spot. And the thick layer of needles that covered the ground would make footprints hard to decipher. He stepped back inside and closed the opening, returning to the library.

Teri questioned him with her eyes. Ian, on the other hand, looked thoughtful.

"He wasn't a ghost."

"No," R.J. agreed.

"Your friend Jacob?" Teri asked.

R.J. inclined his head. "That's my guess."

"Who's Jacob?" Ian wanted to know.

"A friend of the Crossleys," R.J. explained. "He's been helping Will—Mr. Leftcowitz—with a surprise for Mrs. Crossley."

"He's the blond ghost?"

"So it seems. I'm guessing he entered the house this way so he didn't have to turn off the alarm at night."

But even as he said the words, R.J. was unconvinced. Did Will and Kathy know about this?

"What about the chains and the moans?" Ian wanted to know.

"More than likely he was trying to scare you back to bed so he could leave again," Teri told him.

"So he's still here?"

"That's what I intend to find out," R.J. told him. "You're going back to bed."

"I want to meet him."

"Tomorrow."

"But—"

"It's late, Ian," Teri injected. "If your mother wakes up and finds you gone again, she's going to be very upset. Then we'll have to explain everything to her. It could ruin Mrs. Crossley's surprise."

"Teri's right," R.J. agreed, grateful for her quick thinking. He needed the boy out of the way before he confronted Jacob. He'd already scared Ian enough for one night, and R.J. seriously doubted he'd be able to control his temper when he found the other man.

"You'll tell me what he says?" Ian pleaded.

"Promise."

"Come on. I'll walk you up," Teri offered.

"I'm not a baby."

"You certainly aren't, but I'm going up to put some shoes on. My feet are freezing."

"All right," Ian agreed reluctantly.

"Hey Ian, we owe you," R.J. told him.

"You do?"

"Without you, we would never have known about this opening. If Jacob didn't tell Chief Crossley, we will. He needs to know. So thanks."

"Cool."

Teri and R.J. shared a rueful smile.

"I'll go up and put on some shoes."

"I'll do the same. Good night, Ian."

"'Night, R.J."

IT WASN'T UNTIL Ian left her at her door and scurried across the back hall to his own room that Teri remembered why she'd gone downstairs in the first place. Too late to call Ian back and ask if he'd tried her doorknob, but that had to have been the sound that had woken her. Didn't it?

Remembering the sense that someone had been in her room, Teri felt reluctant to step back inside. What if there was another hidden passage in there? What if this Jacob person had used it to come inside and watch her as she slept?

Teri shivered. Taking a deep breath, she entered, turning on all the lights. The room was exactly as she had left it. She quickly pulled on socks and shoes while sliding glances around the walls.

No paneling. No fireplace. Not even any built-in shelves. Why wasn't that more reassuring?

"What are you doing?"

At the sound of R.J.'s voice she spun away from the wall she'd started to examine.

"You scared me!"

"Sorry, but what are you doing?"

Fully dressed, he looked solidly reassuring standing there holding her flashlight and another one of his own.

"Looking for another hidden entrance."

Instead of the amusement she expected, his expression turned worried.

"Why?"

"Because I think someone was in my room tonight while I was sleeping."

He stepped inside and closed the door.

"Why would you think that?"

His eyes glittered with fierce intensity. Only a few hours ago, that expression would have made her uneasy. Now she faced him without a qualm.

"Something woke me. I'm not sure what it was, but I had a feeling...you'll think it's silly."

"No," he said flatly, "I won't. You had a feeling someone had been in here."

"Yes."

He nodded toward the connecting bathroom. "Are you sure—"

"Both the door on my side and the one leading to Mrs. Cosgrove's room were locked."

"Did you leave this closet door ajar?"

She stared at the door, apprehension wrapping itself around her mind. The closet was paneled in cedar.

"I'm not sure."

Stepping past her, R.J. opened the closet and walked inside. "There is a passage in here. Alexis had me seal it off before she opened Heartskeep."

The acid taste of fear washed her mouth as he stepped inside the closet and ran his hand along the bottom of the wall above the baseboard. Soundlessly, a panel of wall slid back, rocking him back on his heels. A gaping black hole was revealed.

"Didn't do a very good job sealing it off, did you?" she managed to say past dry lips.

R.J. swore under his breath. His stark expression held anger when he turned to her.

"Where does it go?" she asked before he could say anything.

"Straight across to Mrs. Cosgrove's closet, up a flight of stairs to a room in the attic and down to the main floor where it connects the two spare bedrooms down there."

She released a deep breath. "What, not all the way to the basement?"

"No."

R.J. flicked on his flashlight and studied the wood he'd nailed in place to prevent this door from opening. Teri could see that someone had pried it free. She couldn't prevent a shiver, particularly when they discovered the opening across from it was still nailed shut.

"Your bedroom's been vacant for a couple of months now," he told her quietly. "Marlene Cosgrove's room has been occupied the whole time."

"Is that supposed to be comforting?"

"It's possible someone was merely using this room as an entrance point."

"Or someone opened it to have a good look at me."

His jaw hardened. "I need to call Wyatt."

"At two o'clock in the morning?"

He hesitated.

"Why don't we see if your friend Jacob or whoever it was opened the doors downstairs?"

"What if it wasn't Jacob?"

"I'll get my gun."

"No!" The word exploded. He rubbed tiredly at his jaw by way of apology. "The last thing I want is a deadly weapon at my back."

"Afraid I'll shoot you?"

"I don't want you shooting anyone." He lowered his voice and gripped her arm. "Where is your gun?"

"Under the mattress so the kids wouldn't find it."

"Could you really shoot a person?"

Teri lifted her head. "If it was him or me, you'd better believe it. You do realize this situation has changed everything."

"What do you mean?"

"If someone is running around Heartskeep at night besides Ian and your friend Jacob," she nodded toward the opening, "this may be the reason Valerie disappeared. She may have seen something she wasn't supposed to see that night."

Chapter Eight

R.J.'s gut twisted. Teri was right. An entirely new scenario had opened and it was one he didn't like thinking about. Something bad was going on at Heartskeep. Again.

"You should wait here while I have a look around."

"As if."

He scowled at her. "I'll give you marks for bravery, but take them away for stupidity. Going in there is a dumb thing to do."

"Don't worry. I won't think any less of you."

"Funny lady. Are you always this bullheaded?"

"What do you think?"

"I think we're probably both crazy."

"Sure you don't want me to get my gun?"

He didn't even have to pause to consider that. "Positive. We'll have a quick look around and come right back."

"What about the library? He could be sneaking out that entrance right now, you know."

"We can only hope," he muttered. "Look, Teri, it's the middle of the night. I don't want a confrontation with anyone. I want to make sure we're safe until morning, and then I'll call Wyatt. We'll just have a quick look around. It's possible Wyatt knows about the library entrance and gave Jacob permission to use it."

"And if he didn't?"

"Then he'll deal with the situation. It's his job, and Jacob is his problem. If you're coming, let's go."

"I still think I should get my gun."

"No guns!"

He had second thoughts about that when they reached the main level. The stops he'd put in place on the two rooms downstairs had been removed as well. Anyone could move freely between the floors without being seen.

"I thought you said this didn't go to the basement."

R.J. spun around. His heart began hammering even before he saw the gaping hole where a section of bare studs and furring had been moved aside to reveal an additional set of stairs he'd never seen before. They disappeared into a maw of inky nothingness.

"They didn't," he told her softly.

"Doesn't look like new construction to me."

He examined the opening. "It isn't. This was built with the house. We never suspected it was here."

"Someone did."

Their eyes met and held. "Yeah."

Teri's voice lowered to a whisper. "We were just down in that basement, R.J. I didn't see a second set of stairs nor any openings in those cinder-block walls, did you?"

"There aren't any," he stated positively. "Wherever this leads, it's no place I've ever been before."

"Someone has."

"Yeah."

He tested the first step with his foot. The wood hadn't rotted, but the handrails on both sides were shakier than he liked. It wouldn't take much to pitch them down the steep, narrow flight of steps.

"If this railing goes, or a step gives out, we're going to fall." He shone the light down into emptiness. "I can't see what's under us."

"Then you'd better go slow."

With a dry look in her direction, he started cautiously down the steps. Teri followed, giving him plenty of lead. Everything around them was dark. The flashlight beam picked nothing out of the emptiness until he was close to the bottom. The stairs ended a short distance before a blank cinder-block wall.

"Not exactly up to code," he muttered, flashing the beam to either side. The light wasn't strong enough to penetrate very far, but the space around them seemed empty in either direction as far as the light could carry. The dank smell of mold was unmistakable.

"I hope you're an aficionado of horror movies," he said quietly, "or you're going to have nightmares about this all night."

"Too late. I think we're having one now. Where are we?"

"Under the right wing of the house. Except that this area was thought to be unexcavated."

"Surprise."

"Uh-huh. I'm guessing the half of the basement we know about is on the other side of this wall." He sent the beam of light around until he picked up more cinder blocks behind them at the outer edge of the light's reach.

"I'd say the space is as wide and as long as the wing above us."

"Makes sense." She inhaled sharply. "What was that?"

"What?" He stilled, straining to listen.

"Something moved over there."

R.J. shone the light in the direction of her pointing arm. He barely caught the reflection of a pair of tiny, beady eyes before the creature skittered out of view.

"Mice."

"You're sure?" Her whisper went up an octave. "It wasn't a rat?"

"Too small. You're not really afraid of mice are you?" Hard to believe this woman was afraid of anything. "They're more afraid of you than the other way around."

"Prove it."

"This is the woman who was willing to bring her gun down here and go up against an unknown person?"

"Person, yes. Mice or rats, no."

"Want to go back upstairs?"

"Yes, so let's hurry and check this place out."

"You aren't going to freak on me, are you?"

"No promises. Just keep that flashlight aimed so we can see them before one charges us."

He nearly chuckled at the image of a charging mouse and closed the distance between them. Humor died when he realized she was trembling.

"Hey, you really are scared. You should go back upstairs."

"I'm fine."

"You're shaking."

"It's pitch-dark, the middle of the night and not exactly what I'd call warm down here. Let's not stand around, okay?"

He cupped the side of her face lightly for a second. "You've got guts."

"I'd rather have my gun. Which way?"

He lowered his hand. "Let's head toward the front of the house first, then we'll work our way back."

"Fine."

R.J. sensed the tension running through her as they started off. Their shoes made little sound on the concrete floor.

"Didn't your brother ever put frogs in your bed?" he asked, trying to distract her.

"I don't have a brother. And if I did have one and he'd been stupid enough to try something like that, I'd have used my gun on him."

R.J. smiled.

"Look!"

There was a path of sorts in the dust that covered the concrete, but it was impossible to tell how many people had walked this way.

"I knew I should have brought my gun," she muttered under her breath.

R.J. was having second thoughts on that issue himself. This was foolish. No one knew where they were. If someone else was down here, anything could happen and they'd disappear—just like Valerie.

He stopped walking. "We need to go back upstairs. I'd say this justifies waking Wyatt in the middle of the night."

"Okay," she agreed quickly.

As he started to turn around, she gripped his arm. "Wait. Look. What's that? An old furnace?"

The flashlight reflected off a large, square metal box. A deeper well of blackness bled off to its right.

"Is that another passage?"

Instead of answering, R.J. headed in that direction. The wall at their side formed a corner right before the metal object.

"That's not a furnace. It's an elevator!"

"It can't be. Can it?"

It was. The scuffed trail of prints led right to it. R.J. circled the metal to find the elevator doors yawning open. Opposite the door was a continuation of the empty basement.

"Where does it go?" she breathed.

"I've no idea, but it runs under the front hall."

Teri shivered. "Do you think there's another exit to the outside?"

The suggestion obviously unsettled him. "I think you should go back upstairs."

"Alone? I don't think so."

"All right. Give me a minute to check this elevator out and then we'll both go."

"You aren't going to get inside that thing!"

He didn't answer. She shivered again. The dark was getting to her. The sound of things skittering away from the flashlight's small beam made her skin crawl. The area was too large, too open and much too empty for her peace of mind. And somehow an elevator in the middle of all this emptiness seemed the scariest part of all.

R.J. kept his voice low as if someone might be nearby listening. The thought made her queasy because it was entirely possible. This vast darkness could hide anything—or anyone.

"Someone's been tinkering with this. You can smell the machine oil."

He was right. She stared as R.J. flashed the light inside the small cage. The beam reflected off something bright red and shiny.

"Is that blood?" she breathed.

He moved closer without answering. Droplets glistened on the control panel and the edge of the door. There were even splotches on the ground.

"Come on," R.J. said harshly. "We're out of here."

"Absolutely."

A sudden grating, scraping noise trapped the breath in her lungs, sending her heart into a frenzy against her rib cage. They both whirled. The sound was coming from the dark stretch of new corridor.

Before her eyes had time to process the fact that the cinder-block wall appeared to be moving, R.J. clicked off his flashlight without a word and then hers, plunging them into total darkness.

He grabbed her arm and tugged silently. Teri allowed him to pull her to the back of the elevator while she thought longingly of the gun tucked out of reach under the mattress upstairs. Someone else was down here, and it was no ghost.

Teri prayed R.J. wouldn't do something heroically stupid as crunching footsteps approached the elevator shaft. The bright beam of a more powerful flashlight bounced about as the person neared. Whoever it was made no effort to be quiet. Obviously he believed he was alone down here. And she was sure from the sound of the footsteps it was a he, not a she.

Metal clanged as something heavy dropped to the concrete. A masculine voice swore. There was another metallic sound. It took Teri a moment to realize that the person was rummaging through a toolbox. Tools made convenient weapons. If the person even began to suspect they were here…

Before she could complete the thought, R.J. breathed a caution in her ear. "Wait here."

There was no time to stop him. R.J. strode around the side of the elevator, making no effort to mask the sound of his approach. She decided if the stranger didn't kill him, she'd do it later—assuming either of them lived to tell the tale.

With a hand on the cold metal as a guide, Teri followed the elevator around to the opposite side, making as little noise as possible.

"Hello, Jacob," R.J. said calmly.

An oath ripped from the other man's throat. "R.J., you nearly scared me to death! What are you doing down here?"

"I was going to ask you the same thing."

Teri peered around the opposite corner. R.J. had the man called Jacob pinned in his flashlight's less powerful beam. Jacob wore a miner's light on his head while a second, much stronger light sat on the ground at his feet, casting a wide glow around the empty space. What sent pure fear through her was the large wrench that glinted in Jacob's hand.

He took a step toward R.J. "Hey, I—"

"Drop the wrench," she ordered without thought. Bunching her fist in the pocket of her slacks like an old-fashioned movie heroine, she stepped forward aggressively, bracing her legs in a classic western pose.

Jacob spun.

"Drop it!" she ordered again. She tried not to squint into the light suddenly blinding her eyes.

"What the—"

R.J. surged forward. Grabbing Jacob, he pinned the arm holding the wrench.

"Let it go, Jacob," he demanded.

The man called Jacob swore, but the wrench dropped to the concrete with a sharp clang as it bounced off the corner of his metal toolbox.

"What are you doing, R.J.? What's going on?"

R.J. released him, sending the man staggering to one side away from the tools. Immediately, R.J. picked up the fallen wrench and stepped out of range.

"Good question, Jacob. I'm sure Wyatt's going to want to know the answer to that when he gets here."

Teri nodded, pleased by the implied threat. Jacob had no way of knowing reinforcements weren't on their way, or that she didn't have a gun in her pocket.

"What are you talking about?" Jacob demanded.

"Gee, I can't imagine," she scoffed.

"Who's she?"

"Don't worry about her. She's not going to shoot you, right, Teri?"

"Not unless he gives me a reason."

"Shoot me?" Jacob glanced back at her. "Are you both nuts? What are you doing, R.J.?"

"Stay where you are," Teri ordered when he took a step toward R.J. R.J. hefted the weight of the wrench as if testing it for balance. Jacob froze at the clearly implied warning.

"This is nuts. What— Oh, wait. I get it. This is about that missing woman, isn't it? I heard she was a friend of yours."

"What do you know about Valerie?"

The quiet menace in R.J.'s voice was enough to raise the hair on the back of her arms.

"Nothing. Not a thing, honest."

"You were here the night she disappeared," Teri commented.

Jacob turned his head quickly in her direction, as if he'd momentarily forgotten about her.

"You were seen," R.J. added.

Jacob swiveled back to R.J. "Of course I was here. I've been here most nights for the past week meeting with Will. I was not only seen, I talked to him. And to Kathy. Ask them. I already told Wyatt I never saw your friend. Neither did Will. I don't know anything about her disappearance."

"There's blood in the elevator," Teri pointed out.

He held up his hand. A large white cloth was wrapped around it. "Mine! I nailed my hand pretty good with the screwdriver trying to take the panel off inside to see if I could make this thing work."

But Teri noticed that his knuckles had a bruised, scraped appearance, as well. From working on the elevator, or a fight with Valerie?

"Why?" R.J. demanded.

"Why what?" Jacob asked, his voice rising. "You mean why try to get the elevator to work? I thought it would make a cool addition to the house, don't you? Kind of an unexpected perk, you know?"

"So Will knows about this."

Instantly, Jacob looked guilty. "Uh, well, no. Not yet. I wanted to surprise him, too."

Teri didn't believe him. It was scary how much he reminded her of Lester, right down to the way he held his head slightly tilted when he spoke. The two men even had that same boyish charm that was so dangerously seductive to the unwary.

Keeping a careful distance from him, Teri edged around to his side for a better view of his face. He glanced her way nervously. R.J. recaptured his attention with another question.

"How did you find all this?"

"That was actually a fluke. I was working my way along the walls in there."

He tossed his head to indicate the cinder-block wall at Teri's back and the known basement on the other side.

"We were trying to figure the best place to excavate for an exit, you know? I was just walking along the wall's perimeter when I dropped my tape measure and spotted one of those catches. You know, like the ones that open the other hidden passages? My first thought was maybe the house already had a secret walkout. It was late and Will had to go, so I didn't say anything to him. I mean, you know all the crazy passages this place has and I didn't know who the girls wanted to know about them, so I decided to come back later on my own and check it out. Instead of a walkout, I found this. Well, actually I found one of the entrances to the other passage down there," he amended pointing in the direction of the side passage.

"There's another opening?" R.J. demanded.

"Yeah. So far I've found three different ones through what we all assumed was a solid wall. They all lead into this hidden section." Enthusiasm built in his tone. "There's one on the other side of the main stairs by that third furnace and hot water heater. I suppose you already saw that."

They hadn't. The equipment must have been on the other side of the stairs toward the back of the house.

"I seem to remember old man Hart replaced the furnaces and the hot water systems shortly before he died. Guess he had the ones in here replaced too, because they look as new as the ones in the main area. Good thing we found them before they needed maintenance, huh? Although, I bet those filters are pretty clogged by now. Lots of dust down here."

"And the hidden staircase to the main floor?" R.J. asked.

"Oh. Well, yeah." He managed to look sheepish. "I was sort of surprised by that one myself. Who would have guessed? The entrance near them was the one I found first."

"How did you find the entrance in the library?" R.J. queried, his tone deceptively neutral.

"You know about that, too?" Jacob grimaced. "I bet it was that kid, right? I was afraid he saw me come in. He nearly gave me a heart attack when he dropped that book. I had no idea anyone was around when I used it tonight. I was in a hurry, so I wasn't as careful as I should have been. The kid didn't blow the surprise, did he?"

"What surprise?"

"You know, what we're doing down here. Did he tell Alexis?"

R.J. shook his head. "Alexis had her baby this morning."

"She did? Hey, that's great. What did she have?"

"A boy," he said flatly.

If Jacob noticed R.J.'s lack of enthusiasm, he ignored it.

"All right! Good for them. Wyatt must be pleased. So if she doesn't know about this yet, we're still clear, right?"

R.J. regarded him with a hard expression. "Why did you open the passages in the closets on the main floor?"

"Oh, that. I wanted to be able to come in through the library and slip down here without being seen. Didn't want to scare all those poor women by walking down the length of the hall late at night."

"The second floor's a long way from the basement," Teri inserted skeptically.

"Second floor? What are you talking about? Who *are* you?"

R.J. shook his head. "She's talking about the closet in Leigh's old bedroom."

"Hey, whoa! I only unblocked the opening to the spare room on the first floor. The one that's closest to the library," he added. "I don't need to go upstairs."

"You're telling us you didn't come into my room tonight while I was asleep?"

"Your room? You're a guest here?"

"Yes or no," she demanded.

"No! Sheesh, I don't even know who you are. I told you, I haven't gone upstairs."

"But you did use the hidden room off the dining room."

Startled, Jacob blinked at her. "Well, yeah. Okay, once. I thought I heard someone and needed to get out of sight fast. How'd you know about that?"

Teri looked at R.J. She didn't want to believe a word he said, but there was a ring of truth to his words.

"Hey, I'm telling you the truth here, R.J."

"If you didn't unblock the openings to the room upstairs, who did?"

"I don't know, but I swear it wasn't me. I only used the hidden stairs to come down here and work on the elevator. And to meet Will," he added.

R.J. gazed at her. Teri raised her shoulders and let them fall. She didn't know Jacob. She figured there was no way for either of them to know how much was true.

"So how did you find the entrance in the library?" R.J. asked.

Again, that sheepish, trust-me grin that raised alarms in her head.

"You know how the girls always said they were going to explore this old place? Well, one day, back before they opened the shelter, I got to thinking about that passage next to the fireplace in the dining room. I figured if there was one secret hiding place, why not two?

I checked out the fireplaces in the living room and kitchen, but they don't have any built-in bookcases, you know? I guess that's the criteria because I hit pay dirt in the library."

Teri eyed him caustically. "And never bothered telling anyone what you'd found."

"Well, no. Okay, I admit it. It was sort of cool knowing a secret like that and not telling anyone else. But I always intended to let the girls know."

"Just another surprise, right?" R.J.'s tone expressed his disbelief as he gave Jacob a hard look.

"Hey, what's got you so bent, man?"

"A friend of mine is missing," he said coldly.

"Well, yeah, okay, but I didn't have anything to do with it."

"How do we know that?" Teri inserted.

"And did it ever occur to you that if you knew a way past the alarm system, someone else might as well?" R.J. demanded.

Jacob's face went slack. While Teri didn't want to believe anything he said, that blank expression would have been hard to fake.

"No," he said hoarsely. "I swear to God, R.J., I never thought of that. But I mean, come on. If Kathy and the girls don't know about the library entrance, who would? Everyone else connected with this place is dead."

"Are they?"

Jacob gawked at him.

"Valerie grew up in Stony Ridge," R.J. told him. "She's about your age, isn't she?"

"Hey, wait a minute!"

"And you said yourself that someone installed a new furnace and hot water tank."

"That means at least one other person knew there was a way through the wall," Teri pointed out. "Who did the installer tell?"

R.J. nodded. "Any number of people might know things about this house that the women and their husbands don't know."

The idea appeared to stun him. Jacob swore softly.

"I never considered that. I swear, R.J. I just figured if Kathy and the girls didn't know, no one else did, either."

Teri wondered if she'd be so quick to disbelieve him if he didn't remind her so strongly of Lester.

"Why are you here now?" she asked.

R.J. nodded approval. "Good question. Why *are* you here?"

"I was supposed to meet with Will earlier only I ran late. I figured he went home because of the weather. Man, there's trees coming down all over the place out there. They got people watching for funnel clouds, for crying out loud! I wasn't about to go driving around once I got here. I thought I'd tinker with the elevator for a while until things calmed down. Then I was going to drive to Lisa's place and crash for the night. She's out of town tonight, but I have a key."

"Lisa?"

"Lisa Striker. We have a…a thing going."

Teri worked to control her temper. "And you think it's perfectly okay to go sneaking around a woman's shelter late at night? I wonder if the people who run this place would agree."

"I'm not *sneaking*. Well, I am in the sense I'm trying not to scare anyone by being seen, but the guys know I've been coming here at night."

"To meet Will for a specific purpose."

"Well, yeah, but this elevator changes everything. I mean, think how much easier it will be for Kathy and Mrs. Norwhich if we can get it up and running. Hey, as long as you're here, do you want to have a look at it with me?"

R.J. hesitated. Teri sensed he wanted to do exactly that. She'd made her point, and she'd make it again when she saw Kathy in the morning. She was pretty sure the other woman wouldn't be pleased to learn Jacob felt free to come and go whenever he liked.

"Have you figured out where the shaft is in relation to the upstairs?" R.J. asked Jacob.

"Yeah. I did a little measuring the other night after everyone was in bed," he replied, excitement returning to his voice. "There's some unaccounted for space between the library and office on the first floor. If I remember correctly, there's some in that front bedroom, too. The one where the Isley woman is sleeping? Of course, I couldn't go in there to confirm, but I'm pretty sure it runs straight up through there."

R.J. nodded. "You're talking about that section of bookcases that jogs out in the library. I never gave that any thought. If I had, I would have figured it was space for the bathroom pipes and vents."

"Too big," Jacob told him. "The void carries into the office as well, but you'd have to measure before you'd realize that."

Teri stiffened as Jacob bent over the toolbox. He lifted the large lantern-style flashlight sitting beside it and started around to her side of the elevator.

"Here. You can see where the plumbing runs up along the shaft."

R.J. followed. Teri edged closer to the toolbox. Bending quickly, she snatched up a screwdriver and stuck it in her pocket. The hammer was tempting but too hard to conceal. She wanted some sort of weapon in case she needed one.

"There are buttons for all three floors," Jacob was saying. "Someone must have paneled over the elevator openings in the halls. I wonder if it opens in the attic."

"Maybe the walls have hidden openings," R.J. suggested.

Jacob was shaking his head as they came back around to the front of the elevator. "I looked. I couldn't find any."

"Did you try riding up in it? Maybe the doors are controlled from inside?"

Teri pursed her lips in exasperation. "Did it ever occur to you two that there might be a reason someone boarded this thing over? Like maybe it's too dangerous to use?"

Jacob grinned unrepentantly. "That's what I've been trying to decide. You're the expert, R.J. What do you think?"

"My expertise doesn't cover elevators."

But Teri could see R.J. was itching for a chance to give it a try. She moved back as the two of them stepped inside the small cage for a closer look.

Moving away from the men, Teri crossed to the cinder-block wall. She hadn't heard Jacob close the opening, but the wall was a solid mass now. Walking to where she thought it had opened, she tapped the surface. Sure felt like solid cinder block.

It took her a few minutes to find the lever near the bottom of the wall that opened the cumbersome door. Once she did, it slid back with a loud grating sound. Both men poked their heads out of the elevator to stare at her.

"What are you doing?" R.J. asked.

"I wanted to see how this worked."

R.J. came forward and lowered his voice. "You all right?"

"Fine. Elevator restoration isn't my thing."

"Mine, either," he agreed ruefully. "We're going to have to hire a professional."

"Uh-huh. Keep it in mind and be careful." She inclined her head toward Jacob who watched from beside the toolbox. "I don't trust him."

R.J. frowned. "You don't believe him?"

"I'm the cautious type."

"You want to head upstairs?"

She didn't answer directly. "I'm just going to prowl around for a minute while you two play."

"Stay nearby," he said after a moment. "Remember the mice."

"I'm not likely to forget. Keep a close watch on him."

He gave her arm a quick squeeze and turned away. Teri hoped he was right about Jacob. She liked R.J., but he was a little too trusting and Jacob was just a little too glib. R.J. wouldn't approve, but she'd made up her mind to run upstairs and get her gun.

The last thing she wanted to do was cross that vast expanse of dark emptiness stretching in front of her, but if she went back the way they had come, R.J. might suspect her intention. The silence of the basement was oppressive. Where was the skittering sound of mice? Even her running footsteps seemed muffled. It was like being swallowed alive down here.

"Stop it," she muttered fiercely. Her flashlight beam was weak but it finally picked up the bottom of the known staircase. She'd grab some fresh batteries for her flashlight as well when she reached her room.

Mounting the steps quickly, she reached for the door handle and twisted. The handle moved, but the door didn't budge. She tried again, putting her weight into it, before she realized the door was locked.

Fear locked her in place. She struggled with a sense of panic. There was no reason to panic. She could go back the way she had come. She was not trapped down here.

Still, she all but ran back down the stairs, pausing at the bottom when an icy coldness passed straight through her. Teri did run then. She was nearly to the far wall when she realized there was no longer an opening showing.

She drew a ragged breath, determined not to drown in the fear that pressed on her. Her heart thumped painfully in her chest as she stared at the seemingly solid bricks. R.J. wouldn't have closed the opening with her on the other side. Besides, the wall made a lot of noise, yet she hadn't she heard it close.

Because Jacob hadn't wanted her to hear.

Chapter Nine

R.J. stepped back, staring at the elevator. "Even if this thing works, we don't want to try running it until we know we won't get stuck between floors and can open it from the inside."

"I suppose you're right," Jacob agreed reluctantly. "I wouldn't want to be trapped in a wall somewhere."

"Or be inside when the cab fell because the cables were faulty."

But R.J.'s mind was no longer on the elevator. Teri hadn't returned. He was starting to understand how her mind worked. She didn't trust Jacob, and he was very much afraid she'd gone upstairs to get her gun.

He didn't completely trust Jacob, either. Why hadn't the other man told anyone about the library entrance? The women staying here were too vulnerable for him to have carte blanche at Heartskeep. R.J. was definitely going to have a long talk with Wyatt.

He turned to look at the wall where Teri had gone and froze. The opening was closed. If there was one thing he was certain of, it was that Teri wouldn't have closed it. Suddenly, her paranoia didn't seem so groundless at all. He spun, grabbing Jacob by the shirtfront and pinned the startled man against the back of the elevator.

"Who's down here with you?" he whispered harshly.

"N-no one. What's wrong with—*uck.*"

R.J. cut off his air. "Last chance. Who's down here with you?"

"No one! I swear!"

"The opening's closed."

"It does that automatically! Honest! It closes on its own. Scared me half to death the first time. It makes all that noise when you open it, but it falls shut on its own without a sound."

"If you're lying to me, I'll break you in half."

Jacob shuddered. "I'm telling you the truth, R.J.!"

"You didn't warn Teri," he growled.

"I forgot!"

"Show me." He thrust Jacob away and picked up the wrench. Jacob stumbled to the wall, fumbling to get it open.

Teri would be thoroughly frightened by now, alone in the dark with only a flashlight and the mice she feared. As soon as she was safe, he was going to pummel Jacob.

The hidden door scraped loudly as it opened.

"Teri!" R.J. called.

There was no answer.

"If she's still down here—"

"Oh, she's still down here," Jacob assured him. "Unless she's got a key. The basement door is locked from the kitchen side."

"I'll deal with you in a minute. Teri! It's okay. I've got Jacob."

"You've got me? What does that mean?" The other man's eyes widened as R.J.'s voice echoed off the concrete walls.

"I don't see her," Jacob said nervously. "Maybe she used one of the other doors."

"She did, you spineless bastard."

R.J. whirled at the sound of her voice. Teri stood beside the elevator, one hand in her pocket, the other holding the flashlight. The light shook. Badly.

His surge of relief sent him to her. She met him halfway and it seemed perfectly natural to pull her into his arms. He felt the tremors quaking her.

"Easy. Take it easy. You're okay now."

"I thought he'd killed you. I was going to shoot him," she lied, wishing she had gone for her gun after all.

"Me?" Jacob squeaked. "What's the matter with you two? Are you both nuts?"

"You locked me in!" she accused, pulling back slightly.

R.J. didn't let her go. There were sunken hollows beneath her eyes, while the ghost of remembered fear lingered in her gaze. She must have been terrified, trapped in the basement like that. Yet she'd come to rescue him instead of fleeing upstairs when she'd had the chance.

Keeping his arm around her shoulders, he turned in time for his flashlight to pick up the concrete opening sliding silently closed at Jacob's back.

"It closes by itself," R.J. told Teri gently. "See?"

"Why didn't he tell me that?"

"I forgot, all right? Sue me," Jacob protested. "Sheesh. You two really are bughouse."

R.J. stared at him. "We're going upstairs to have a long chat with Wyatt. We've explored more than enough for one night."

"Fine by me. At least he's not crazy."

"Lead the way."

"Where is your coat?" Teri asked as they followed Jacob toward the hidden set of stairs.

R.J. maintained an arm around her. She didn't seem to mind.

"My coat?"

"It's been storming outside. You didn't come here without wearing one."

"It's upstairs. I left it in the connecting bathroom on the main floor. In the tub," he added with exaggerated patience as they started up the rickety stairs single file, "behind the shower curtain where no one would see it. I didn't want to drip all over the house or Kathy would kill me."

"You should search his pockets when we get upstairs," Teri whispered at his back.

Jacob turned around sharply. "For what?"

"Weapons," she snapped.

"You mean like a gun? Sheesh, R.J., I can't believe she's for real. Why would I be carrying a gun?"

"So you could shoot someone?"

"R.J., look man, I don't know who this woman is and I'm not real sure what's going on here, but I'm not part of whatever it is, all right? All I'm trying to do is give the girls a present. I owe them. But I gotta tell you, if creating this center means more trouble for me, I'm out of here, debt or no debt. I've had enough trouble to last me a lifetime."

R.J. nodded. Teri shot him an incredulous look, but R.J. believed Jacob. Despite several unanswered questions, he was convinced Jacob was telling them the truth.

"Teri's a private investigator. She's looking into Valerie's disappearance," he explained. "I think someone else knows about the library," he added to Teri.

"But—"

"She won't sleep until she checks your pockets, all right?"

Jacob swore. The curse sounded more resigned than angry.

"Fine. Check my pockets. Go out and check my car. Just get me the heck out of here."

"You aren't going home tonight."

"You think I want to stay here with a couple of nutcases like the two of you?"

"The roads are blocked by flooding."

"I'll make it," Jacob assured him as they reached the top of the stairs. "At least to Lisa's place."

Tension radiated through Teri.

"No!" She quivered, but faced Jacob with fierce intensity. "You don't drive through standing water. Not ever."

"Wha—"

"Teri's from Texas," R.J. said in sudden understanding. "They get a lot of flash floods down there, don't they?"

She shivered, but didn't take her eyes off Jacob. "People die from driving into standing water. It takes very little to sweep a car away."

There was such an undercurrent of emotion in her voice that R.J. squeezed her shoulders gently while he wondered who she'd lost in such a way.

"It's late, Jacob. We're all tired. You can use the other spare bedroom for what's left of the night. I'm in here."

"No he can't. Will's in there, remember?"

"Nah," Jacob grinned. "That may be what he said, but he doesn't sleep alone when he sleeps over."

R.J. remembered what Ian had said about Will and

Kathy and shifted uncomfortably. "Okay, well, give me your word you'll hang around in the morning and talk to Wyatt."

"You'd trust my word?"

"Yes." He didn't look at Teri, knowing she'd disapprove.

Jacob nodded. "All right then, I'll see you in the morning, but you have to do the explaining to Kathy. Help yourself to my coat. And Teri, for the record, I had nothing to do with Valerie's disappearance, but I can tell you one thing. This house is cursed. Bad things happen at Heartskeep. If it was up to me, I'd pull the place down, burn it and scatter the ashes. And on that note, sleep well, you two."

R.J. watched him open the hidden catch and step into the opposite spare bedroom without a backward glance.

"You trust him?"

"I believe him," R.J. corrected. "Come on. We'll check his coat."

The coat was where he'd claimed, an expensive, full-length black leather with a set of keys in one pocket and a gasoline receipt in the other. The bathroom also contained a wet washcloth with traces of blood. Teri said nothing. R.J. could see her exhaustion.

"It's been a long night. I'll walk you to your room."

She shook her head, her gaze imprisoning his. "I don't think I could sleep up there knowing…"

"Would you like stay here? We can share the bed. There's plenty of room and I don't snore."

She eyed him steadily. "I'm not looking for sex, R.J."

"Didn't think you were, more's the pity. Do you want the right or left side?" He told his libido to calm down. This wasn't about sex.

"Either one."

"I'll take the right, then." It was closer to the door. Anyone who came in tonight would have to go through him to get to her.

While the thought felt melodramatic, he wasn't going to let anyone hurt her if he could prevent it. And if that made him a chauvinist, so be it.

There was nothing the least bit sexy about a woman in a sweatsuit, still, R.J. was totally aware of Teri's body next to his in the queen-size bed. Despite his exhaustion, he knew he'd never fall asleep.

After several minutes of trying to lie still, he realized Teri wasn't faring any better.

"Did you know someone who was caught in a flash flood?" he asked quietly. It was a stupid question. He was pretty sure he already knew the answer, and all it would do was dredge up old memories she'd probably rather not face.

She didn't respond for so long that he thought she wasn't going to answer. He was almost relieved.

"Yes," she replied so softly he could barely hear her answer.

"I'm sorry."

Why had he asked? He'd known it had to be something like that. He heard a shuddery breath and felt guilty for pushing her. "Come here."

To his complete surprise, she rolled toward him. He put his arm around her and felt her tremble.

"I'm so tired," she whispered.

"Me, too. It'll be morning in a couple of hours."

"We should—"

"Sleep," he told her firmly. "Nothing else is going to happen tonight."

Green eyes blinked up at him. The ghost of a smile

flickered there. His body stirred. He told it to settle down.

"Nothing," he promised. "As tempting as you are, I don't think I could summon the energy for more than holding you tonight." His body called him a liar.

She closed her eyes on a smile. He kissed the top of her head. With a soft sigh, she laid her cheek against his shoulder.

R.J. closed his own eyes and stroked the softness of her hair. He woke to a watery sunlight spilling across the bed.

Teri was cradled spoon-style against his body. His hand was cupping her breast, and his body was hard. Sharing the bed last night had been about comfort. This morning, his body was ready for sex.

He knew the second her eyes opened. She became rigid. He withdrew the offending hand and rolled over on his back, oddly embarrassed.

"'Morning," he muttered.

Teri rolled away before turning to face him. The vulnerability in her unguarded expression went straight to his gut. Her features changed in the next heartbeat, and he realized how much he hated that bland, empty expression she generally kept in place.

"Good morning. I can't believe I actually slept. What time is it?"

He had to look twice at his watch before he believed the display. "Eight-thirty-seven." He sat up and swung his legs to the floor, hoping she didn't notice the erection pressing against the inside of his jeans.

"I can't remember the last time I was in bed this late."

"Well, we didn't go to sleep until after three."

"True. You want to use the bathroom first?"

"Go ahead." She slipped out of bed. "I'll use the hidden stairs to go up to my room."

He tried for humor. "Afraid to be seen coming out of my room at this hour?"

She reached a hand up to her hair. "Afraid to be seen, period."

He met her near the foot of the bed. "You look beautiful."

"Liar."

"Beauty's more than hair and makeup." The words surprised him as much as her, but it was true. Disheveled and sleep-kissed, she was lovely.

"You're a nice man, R.J. Monroe."

"Keep it under your hat. I'm going for the dark, dangerous image."

Her lips turned up. "Not happening. Not anymore."

"Darn. I'll work on it."

Her smile widened.

"Are you okay?"

Color tinted her cheeks. "Fine. I, uh, I want to thank you. For last night. I'm not usually so—"

"Bold? Brave?"

"Stupid."

"Hey." He stroked her cheek with the tips of two fingers. "Thanks aren't necessary between friends."

The smile wobbled, but held. "I'd better go."

He studied her face. "If you don't want me to kiss you, that's probably true."

Her eyes widened. "Morning breath."

"I'm willing to risk it. More than likely, we'll cancel each other."

She flattened her hands against his chest as he started to lean in toward her. "Toothpaste."

"Spoilsport." But he stepped back, smiling, feeling

lighter than he had in years. He liked sparring with Teri. "You okay to go up there by yourself?"

"Despite last night's performance, I'm fine."

"You are at that."

Her lips parted in surprise.

"Get."

"Going."

He stuck his head inside the hidden area and watched until she was upstairs and in her room. He wondered what she would have said if he'd invited her to share his shower.

IAN HID IN THE GYM, dodging Mrs. Drexler while he waited for Teri or R.J. to wake up and tell him what had happened last night. No one was acting weird downstairs, so it seemed they didn't know about this Jacob person being in the house.

He was sort of sorry to learn he hadn't been seeing a ghost after all. Maybe his mother was right. Maybe there was no such thing, but it was cool to think there might be ghosts.

As anxious as he was to tell Nola and Boone about the hidden entrance in the library, he hadn't been able to get them alone. He'd been lucky to slip away after breakfast before Mrs. Drexler caught him and dragged him off to the playroom for more math.

He had a new concern this morning. His mother was definitely acting all scared again and he didn't know why. She was trying to hide it, but he could tell. She'd been on her cell phone early this morning and the person on the other end must have said something to upset her. He was pretty sure it hadn't been *him*, but he was also sure she was going to tell him they were leaving again. Two days ago, that would have been good news. Today, he wanted to stay and explore some more.

Hearing voices in the main hall, Ian slipped out of the gym and hurried to the back staircase. He intended to hide in his bedroom, but a wave of intense cold made him back against the wall near the corner bedroom Corey's mother had used before she disappeared.

Someone began crying inside. Except this room was supposed to be empty.

Ian pressed his ear to the door. The sound broke off midsob.

Fear and excitement gripped him. He reached out and tried the doorknob. The handle twisted but stopped. Locked.

Had Corey's mother come back?

Lightly, Ian tapped on the wood door. "Hello?"

Silence.

"Is someone in there?"

"What are you doing?" Mrs. Walsh asked.

Startled, he spun to face her. "There's someone in there."

"No there isn't."

"I heard a woman crying."

Mrs. Walsh got a funny look on her face.

"Move away from the door, Ian."

He did, and she inserted her key in the lock. Ian followed her in, but the room was clearly empty. Walking to the bathroom, she stepped inside and pulled back the shower curtain, revealing an empty tub. The closet was empty as well.

"There's no one in here, Ian."

She sounded almost relieved.

"I heard someone," he insisted.

Mrs. Walsh laid a hand on his shoulder. "This old

house plays lots of acoustical tricks. Sometimes sound travels in the strangest ways. You probably heard Mrs. Cosgrove or Mrs. Isley."

"They're clear on the other side of the house," he protested. "What I heard came from in here."

"I'm sure that's what it sounded like, dear, but it couldn't have been. You can see the room is empty."

"It could have been a ghost," he told her defiantly.

That funny look came and went on her face again, as if she knew something scary and wasn't going to tell. But she shook her head and ushered him out into the hall.

"If it was, it's gone now. And we need to go as well. Mrs. Drexler is looking for you."

Ian wouldn't let it rest.

"There was something real cold in the hall right before I heard the crying."

As she relocked the door, he saw her fingers weren't quite steady.

"Do *you* think it could have been a ghost?"

He expected her to deny it, but she surprised him by turning around and regarding him seriously.

"Ian, if ever a place has earned the right to be haunted, it's Heartskeep. Good and bad things have happened here over the years, but ghosts can't hurt you."

"So that was a ghost?"

"I can't say. I can only tell you there are many unexplained noises and cold spots in this house. But they've never harmed anyone. Now run along to the playroom. Mrs. Drexler wants to get your studies started this morning."

He wanted to protest, except that she'd practically admitted there were ghosts here at Heartskeep. So maybe this Jacob person had been the figure he'd seen in the library, like R.J. said, but then again, maybe it had been a ghost.

Ian hurried down the hall. He couldn't wait to tell Nola and Boone.

R.J. UNLOCKED THE door to the connecting bath and knocked before entering. When no one called out, he opened the door. Not only was the bathroom empty, it looked exactly as it had last night.

Except that Jacob's coat was gone.

That spurred him to the opposite door. He knocked even as he twisted the handle. The spare bedroom was empty. There was no sign that the bed had been slept in. Jacob had taken his coat and left.

With a curse, R.J. hurried back to his room and reached for his cell phone. His call to Wyatt went straight through to voice mail. Frustrated, he left a message and hung up. He shouldn't have been so trusting. Jacob must have skipped out as soon as R.J. and Teri closed the connecting door to the bedroom. There was little consolation in telling himself there was nothing he could have done to prevent it.

He showered and shaved quickly, knowing Teri would be upset that Jacob was gone. She'd been right not to trust Jacob. But what was the man up to?

The minute he was dressed, he used the phone to call Doc's office to check on Lucky.

"He's doing great, R.J.," Marion told him. "He'll have to take things easy for a few days, but I think by this evening he'll be more than ready to go home. Give us a call later this afternoon."

"Thanks, Marion. I really appreciate it."

He decided to use the hidden staircase to Teri's room to prevent running into someone and being delayed by questions. The closet door in Teri's room was shut, so he knocked. It seemed weird to be knocking on the inside of a closet door, but he didn't want to barge into the room and embarrass her if she was getting dressed.

There was no answer. R.J. hesitated a moment before entering the room.

"Teri?"

The sound of running water stopped and she stepped from the bathroom at the sound of his voice. Dressed in a pair of black jeans and another black turtleneck, her head was wrapped in a towel, a tube of moisturizer in her hand. She looked sleek and sexy and dangerously alluring. Sky-blue eyes gazed at him in alarm.

"R.J.? What's wrong?"

"Nothing. Well, Jacob split. The bed wasn't slept in, so he must have gone as soon as we left him. I tried to call Wyatt— Wait a minute. Blue eyes?"

Panic flared in their depths for an instant.

"I wear green contact lenses," she growled. "What happened when you tried to call Wyatt?"

His stomach knotted. "Why?"

"Because I'd like to know what he said about Jacob!"

"No. I mean why green contact lenses?"

She gave him an exasperated look, but every line of her body radiated tension.

"I need them to see."

"But why green ones?"

"Vanity," she snapped. "Will you get on with it?"

She was lying. If there was one thing he felt certain of, it was that Teri didn't have a vain bone in her body.

"So the red hair isn't real, either?"

She paled. "I am not going to stand here and discuss

my makeup choices with you. Go away and let me finish getting dressed."

Pivoting, she stepped into the bathroom and shut the door with a finality that echoed louder than if she'd slammed it.

All his earlier concerns returned. Who *was* Teri Johnson?

TERI FOUND IT HARD to regain her composure. She knew better than to let her guard down, but her eyes had been so irritated this morning she hadn't wanted to put fresh lenses in. She hated wearing contacts.

Still, she'd overreacted. What did it matter if R.J. knew she dyed her hair and wore green contact lenses? Lots of women did. She should have dismissed it instead of acting defensive. She'd undoubtedly made him suspicious. That would only make things harder for her. She needed R.J. She had to convince him to take her to Corey.

She swore at her reflection in the bathroom mirror as she smeared lotion over her face and wondered how to rectify the situation.

Darn it, she didn't have time to worry over what R.J. thought of her. With any luck, she'd find out where Corey was and be away from here by midafternoon.

And she'd never see R.J. Monroe again.

So what? Nothing could happen between them even if she wasn't leaving. He was a means to an end, that was all.

Too bad she couldn't bring herself to flirt and play coy. She'd bet one of his usual women would have had the information she needed in short order. What was it Alexis had called him? Stony Ridge's favorite bachelor?

Yeah. Right. Teri was exactly his type.

Tugging the towel from her hair, she forced her mind to study the tousled wreck. Too wet to style, and it would take forever to blow-dry. R.J. would be waiting for her downstairs with his suspicions fully aroused.

The mystery here at Heartskeep was distracting her from her goal—find Corey and get away as quickly as possible.

Toweling moisture from her hair, she braided the wet strands quickly, knowing she'd pay with tangles later. Putting on socks, she slid her feet into a dry pair of Loafers before selecting a fresh pair of contacts. Her eyes protested, but she got them in. In the bedroom, her cell phone began to ring. Olivia, of course. She was the only one who had this number.

Teri threw open the bathroom door, shocked to find R.J. still waiting in the room. He stood at the bedroom window with his back to her. She hesitated. The phone stopped ringing as the call switched to voice mail.

"Another storm?" she asked, hating the nervous quaver in her voice as she joined him at the window.

He turned. "Not yet, but it looks like it may start raining again any second."

She tried to relax and failed. She hated storms. Hated them!

R.J. studied her expression with a frown. She had to get control of herself. He was far too perceptive. And he was standing much too close for comfort.

"We should go down and join the others for breakfast," she told him nervously.

He reached for her hand. The contact brought a shiver of unwanted reaction. Though she immediately pulled free, his touch remained imbedded in her skin.

"I want to apologize. I had no right to make personal

comments, Teri. My only excuse is that your real eye color caught me by surprise."

His sincerity caused a gut reaction she hadn't anticipated. She could not afford to be this attracted to R.J. Too bad her hormones weren't getting the message. She inhaled the clean scent of soap and managed a quick step back.

"No big deal. I know it's vain, but I always wanted red hair and green eyes."

Aware of his gaze on her, she turned away and lifted her cell phone. Checking the number to confirm it had been Olivia, she switched the ring to vibrate and clipped the phone to her slacks.

"Do you need to return that call?"

"Yes, but I'll do it after breakfast. I'm starving," she lied. "Let's go eat."

She stepped briskly into the hall, leaving R.J. little choice but to follow. Despite his apology, she could see the questions in his gaze. In the process of trying to avoid them, she nearly ran into Kathy as the older woman came around the corner.

"Oh, good. You're awake. I was just coming to check on the two of you."

She assumed they had spent the night together? Well, they had, but not in the way she was thinking.

R.J. didn't even blink. "Is something wrong, Kathy?"

"The front gate was destroyed last night."

"What?"

"How?" Teri asked.

"Will says it looks like the storm took down one of the large trees and drove the trunk right through the gate. The whole mangled mess was shoved clear across the road. Bram's going to have rebuild that beautiful gate."

"I'll go out and give Will a hand," R.J. told her immediately.

Kathy stopped him with a shake of her head. "There's nothing you can do. Everything is clear of the road, so it isn't a safety hazard."

"Can we get up and down the driveway?"

"Oh, yes. That isn't blocked at all."

"It isn't protected anymore, either," Teri pointed out.

Kathy looked momentarily disconcerted.

"Well, I don't think we'll have to worry about trespassers for a while anyhow. Most of the major roads around us are under water. And they're calling for more storms, if you can believe it."

Teri believed it, though that was one piece of news she didn't want to hear.

"Have you seen Jacob this morning?" R.J. asked Kathy.

"Jacob? No. Why?"

"We caught him prowling around the house about two o'clock this morning. He was supposed to spend the night in the spare room. You didn't know he was here?"

"No." Flustered, she managed to look both shocked and worried as Kathy realized for certain that they knew Will hadn't used that room the night before. "Will expected him earlier last night, but he never showed up."

R.J. nodded. "Do you know of any other secret entrances or exits to Heartskeep?"

The older woman's eyes widened in alarm. "No. Only that one they found after the fire a couple of years ago," she amended. "And you dismantled what was left of that when you turned the ballroom into a gym."

"Jacob found another one in the library."

The back of her hand went to her mouth. "We need to tell Wyatt."

"I tried to reach him a few minutes ago."

Kathy shook her head. "I spoke with him after Will discovered the gate was destroyed. Wyatt was leaving for the hospital to pick up Alexis and the baby, so I told him there was no urgency coming out here."

"There isn't," R.J. assured her. He laid a comforting hand on her shoulder, but his expression told Teri he wasn't happy with this news.

"You don't think Jacob had anything to do with Valerie's disappearance, do you, R.J.?" Kathy asked worriedly.

"I don't know. Jacob's keeping secrets, and I'd like to know why. He promised to spend the night in the room next to mine and wait here to talk with Wyatt this morning, but the bed wasn't slept in."

"Maybe he went home," was all Kathy said.

"It's a long way to the interstate with so many roads flooded."

"Maybe he went to The Inn," she suggested.

"He said he has a girlfriend living nearby, didn't he?" Teri interjected.

"That's right," R.J. agreed. "Don't worry about it, Kathy. We'll let Wyatt handle Jacob."

"Do you think the women are safe?" she asked urgently.

"From Jacob? Yeah. I think so."

"I hadn't thought about possible danger with the gate down. What should we do?"

"Keep the house alarm set and keep everyone busy and together as much as possible. Where's Will?"

"Outside cleaning up the storm debris."

"I'll give him a hand."

"After breakfast," Kathy said firmly.

Mrs. Norwhich was more wraithlike and truculent than ever as she prepared them a late breakfast Teri had no appetite for. The ominous clouds outside darkened everyone's mood as a new storm moved in.

R.J. tried to coax a smile from Mrs. Norwhich to no avail. As soon as she could, Teri carried her dishes to the sink and told R.J. she was going down the hall to return the earlier phone call. She was aware that his troubled gaze followed her as she left.

The office next to the library was vacant, so she stepped in there and took a seat behind the lovely old desk as rain splattered the windows. Olivia answered on the first ring, frantic with worry. She'd been watching The Weather Channel and had seen the reports of the flooding in the New York area. She'd been terrified when she'd been unable to reach Teri.

Teri soothed her, explaining she was safe, but temporarily stranded at Heartskeep.

"What about Corey?"

"I'm working on it."

"You're running out of time, Teri."

"Tell me something I don't know."

"You have to get to Corey before Lester does," Olivia fretted.

Teri's resolve hardened. "I intend to. Is there any change in..?"

"No. Your sister is still in a deep coma. You know the odds aren't good, Teri. Even if she comes out of it…"

"She's going to come out of it. And she's going to be all right," Teri insisted. She refused to consider any other possibility. "And I'm going to find Corey one way or another."

A sudden prickle of awareness stiffened her spine. Without looking toward the hall, she knew R.J. stood in the doorway. How much had he heard?

"I have to go. I'll call you later." Teri disconnected without waiting for Olivia's response.

Her heart thudded as she faced him. His features were inscrutable.

"I didn't mean to interrupt, but Lester Boyington is here."

Her heart leaped to the back of her throat before it began to thunder against the wall of her chest. "What do you mean, he's here?"

"He's coming up the driveway right now."

Panic filled her. "How do you know?"

"Will met him out front and used his cell phone to alert Kathy. Don't worry. I can handle him."

She flew across the room, grabbing his arm. "You can't give him Corey. Promise me!"

"I can't give him what I don't have," he said stiffly. "Corey isn't here."

"Don't tell him where Corey is."

His gaze bore into her.

"He *is* Corey's father, isn't he?"

Her lips felt numb. Her voice was strained as she answered. "Yes, but he tried to kill Corey's mother."

"We don't know that."

He was wrong. *She* knew that better than anyone. Only there wasn't time to explain anything to him now. Lester was here!

"R.J., you have to trust me. Don't tell him where Corey is. Please!"

He removed her hand from his arm without expression. "It isn't my place to tell him anything, Teri. I'm going to refer him to Wyatt. Wait here."

He was coldly furious, she realized. She should have trusted him sooner. Maybe if she'd told him the truth, he would have helped her. R.J. was a good person, an honorable man. Surely he wouldn't be deceived by Lester.

"Teri?"

Ian hesitated in the door between the office and the library. His features were pale and tight with concern. She crossed to him, fear quickening her pace.

"What's wrong, Ian?"

"There's a man coming up the front steps."

"I know."

She should tell him it was all right, that everything was going to be okay. But she couldn't summon the words.

"He looks like the blond ghost," Ian told her as R.J. answered the front door.

Chapter Ten

Lester Boyington stood in the hall, his expensive gray topcoat dripping water, his thinning blond hair plastered to his scalp. His boyishly handsome face puckered apologetically as he stared around at his reception committee.

Kathy Walsh stood beside R.J. to greet him. Janet Isley and Marlene Cosgrove watched from the opening to the living room. Betty Drexler, Evelyn Sutter, Nola and Boone were paused partway down the front staircase.

Lester cast his glance around the sea of nervous faces, coming to land on hers before she could take a step back into the library. To Teri's profound relief, he dismissed her with a cold sweep of his eyes and focused his attention on R.J. Will opened the front door and stepped inside behind him.

Teri realized her hand rested protectively on Ian's shoulder. She didn't remove it.

"Who is that?" he whispered without looking away.

Somehow, she managed to force the words past her dry throat. "Corey's father."

"I don't like him."

The firmly spoken words snapped her self-induced

sense of panic. She gave his shoulder a tender squeeze. "Me, either."

"I knew the storms were bad up this way, but I had no idea how bad," Lester was saying to R.J. and Kathy. He moved stiffly forward as if holding himself carefully.

"I didn't have the radio on driving up here because I was in a small car accident the other day and I didn't want to risk another distraction in this weather.

"Look, I'm sorry to barge in on you this way but I didn't learn about Valerie until late last night. I've been in Chicago on business all week. After I spoke with Chief Hepplewhite this morning, I was so distraught I got in my car and drove up here immediately."

The back of her throat hurt with the force of her emotions. She wanted to shout a warning to them all, to tell them not to be deceived by his words. But she sensed it was already too late. Lester knew exactly how to play to a crowd.

"Where's my son? Where's Corey?"

"I'm sorry, Mr. Boyington," Kathy replied, "Corey isn't here."

"The chief of police had him placed in foster care after his mother disappeared," R.J. inserted.

Lester looked crestfallen. "I thought…"

He shrugged and she saw the smallest wince of pain. Had he really been in an accident? The dark side of her hoped so.

"It doesn't matter what I thought," he continued. "Was she all right? Valerie, I mean. Did she look all right?"

"She'd been beaten," Kathy told him flatly.

"Oh, God."

His look of devastation was perfect. Teri would have believed him herself if she hadn't known better.

"What about Corey? Was he...? Is he all right? No one hurt him, did they?"

His appearance of genuine anguish would have netted him a standing ovation if this had been a stage, but this audience didn't seem to realize he was giving a performance. Kathy hastened forward to lay a comforting hand on his sleeve.

He stepped away from the touch without making it obvious by turning to face her. Kathy was unaware of the intended slight. She went on in a rush.

"Corey is fine. Valerie was very protective of the boy. She took excellent care of him."

"Can you tell me where he is?"

Teri's eyes narrowed. He was definitely holding himself stiffly as if it pained him to move. Somehow, she didn't think that was part of his act.

"Sorry," R.J. inserted before Kathy could respond. "You'll have to speak with our chief of police. When your wife disappeared, Corey couldn't stay here alone. Rules, you understand. This is a family shelter. We aren't prepared to keep small children without their mothers."

Kathy stared at R.J. in obvious surprise. But if she was upset to have her authority usurped by what was, after all, nothing more than a local carpenter for hire, she didn't challenge R.J.

The flash of annoyance came and went on Lester's face so fast Teri doubted anyone besides her had noticed. He managed a sad smile that didn't touch the hardness of his cold eyes.

"I see. It's just that this whole thing... Well, it's all come as something of a shock. I thought Val was finally getting better. She seemed happy. I travel a lot in my job and, well... I should have quit. Found something else. But we needed the money and… I'm sorry. I'm rambling. It's just that I didn't discover Valerie had this…drug problem until after we were married."

Teri made a fist.

"It caused some problems at first, but I honestly thought she had it under control after we moved to the country. The move was her idea, you see. Going somewhere to make a fresh start. We figured she was safe from drug pushers in a place like Fools Point. And she hardly ever went into town. I kept encouraging her to make friends, but…"

He closed his eyes as though in pain. Teri could barely contain an urge to run into the hall and shake him until he told the truth. But, of course, he wouldn't. He'd just turn those sad, concerned eyes on her and continue to lie through his too-white teeth.

And his audience was buying into every word he uttered. Teri saw sympathetic expressions on the faces of all the women gathered around the huge foyer. She controlled an urge to shout at them. They were abused women. They should have known better! But even R.J. appeared to be moved by the performance.

Ian glanced up at Teri. "He's lying," he whispered.

His words were an unexpected balm. She forced the fingers of her right hand to relax, but she didn't drop her other hand from his shoulder, giving it a reassuring squeeze instead.

"Yes," she agreed. "He certainly is."

As if drawn by their quiet exchange, Lester raised his head. His dark eyes swept the two of them from head to toe.

A helpless wash of pure panic froze her in place.

With a dismissive narrowing of his eyes, Lester looked away again. It seemed like minutes passed before she could breathe again. He didn't like redheads, she reminded herself. He didn't like busty women.

And he didn't know who she was.

"Are you okay, Teri?"

She exhaled shakily. "Yes," she assured the child and found R.J.'s thoughtful gaze moving away from the two of them as well.

"If you could direct me to the police station," Lester was saying as his gaze lingered on Evelyn's battered face a moment, "I'll collect my son and take him home. I want to thank you for looking after him and my wife. I know you did the best you could to keep them safe."

The tiny implication being that their best had been sadly lacking but he wouldn't hold it against them.

"I'll walk you out and give you directions," R.J. offered.

"Thank you. I'd appreciate it."

He sent a final gaze over the faces as if committing them to memory. Teri felt the hair lift at the back of her neck as it passed over her and Ian. Then he was gone, and everyone turned away.

Nola and Boone joined Ian and her in the library. The others collected in a knot in the hall.

"He looked like the blond ghost," Nola said excitedly.

Teri nodded.

"Does he look like Jacob?" Ian asked her.

"Yes. He does."

It was true insofar as their height and coloring and general shape. But Jacob lacked Lester's dark intensity.

"Who's Jacob?" Nola demanded.

"Did you find him last night?" Ian asked at the same time.

"Yes. He's the one you saw."

"Who's Jacob?"

"A friend of Wyatt's," Teri explained.

Ian frowned. "So he was trying to scare me by making all that noise?"

"No. Actually, he was working on something in the basement and hurt himself. The noise must have carried up through the pipes."

She was rather proud of that explanation, but Ian looked momentarily depressed. Then he brightened.

"Well, he isn't the one I heard crying in Corey's room."

The air was suddenly sucked from her lungs. "When?"

"A little while ago. Mrs. Walsh opened the door, but the room was empty. Even she said Heartskeep is probably haunted," he added triumphantly, gazing at Nola.

"Show me," Teri commanded.

"I can't. She locked the door again."

"I know where they keep a spare key," Nola said abruptly, then shrugged as if uncomfortable for saying anything. "I saw Mrs. Norwhich put it on a hook in the kitchen utility closet a few days ago."

Teri was torn. Every instinct demanded she go to R.J. as soon as he came back inside and force him to tell her where Corey was. But she couldn't do that in front of everyone at Heartskeep. Besides, she wasn't sure he'd tell her anything now. While she knew she shouldn't involve the children, this was the perfect time for a quick look inside Valerie's room.

What if there was a secret passage in that bedroom, as well? Her heart was a trip-hammer of excitement.

What if Valerie had never left Heartskeep?

The children, of course, wanted to come with her.

Teri was trying to figure out how to discourage them after Nola slipped into the kitchen and stolen the key when the problem was solved by Evelyn Sutter. The woman spotted the four of them heading up the back staircase.

"There you are! Mrs. Drexler and I have been looking all over for you. Mrs. Norwhich is going to have lunch ready early. Then we need to go upstairs and finish your schoolwork."

"I'm not hungry. Can't it wait, Mom?" Ian protested. "We were going to go do something."

"Lunch," she said firmly. "All of you."

"Actually, I just had a late breakfast," Teri told her. "Please tell Mrs. Norwhich I'm skipping lunch."

"She won't be happy, you know."

"I think that's normal for her."

Evelyn Sutter's lips quirked. "All right, then. The rest of you get washed up right now." But her eyes sent a question at Teri.

Teri realized she couldn't leave without speaking to the woman. "Maybe after lunch we could have a cup of coffee together."

Evelyn nodded, relief obvious in her expression.

"Yes, I'd like to speak with you. I'm afraid I've done something extraordinarily foolish."

Teri frowned in concern. She had a feeling Evelyn was ready to bolt, and, frankly, she thought that might be the smart thing to do at this point.

"All right. I'll find you in a little while. And I'll talk to you guys after lunch," Teri told the children.

They looked unhappy, but none of them gave her away.

Upstairs, all was silent. Teri inserted the key in the lock of the corner bedroom and it turned with a soft snick. Twisting the handle, she started to open the door. The door slammed shut against her, as if someone were standing on the other side pushing it closed. Releasing the handle, she took an inadvertent step back. Coldness washed over her as the door swung open.

Heart pounding, she stood where she was, surveying the bleak room beyond. Despite the size of the heavy dark wood pieces, the furniture seemed lost in the large bedroom. Teri was instantly thankful she hadn't been assigned to this room. There was a brooding, masculine feel in here that made her shudder.

She saw nothing that would account for the way the door had slammed shut against her, but it hadn't been her imagination. Could this door be like the one in the basement that closed itself? But this one had then opened.

"Hello? Anyone in here?"

Silence.

As she crossed the threshold, a quiver of unease scooted down her spine. Though the drapes were open, the room was dark. Rain drove relentlessly against the windowpanes, and thunder echoed distantly overhead.

The door to the bathroom gaped open. Teri approached cautiously, ready to run. The room was empty. To her surprise, this bathroom didn't connect to the room next door. A huge closet opened off the bath instead. That door was partially ajar, as well. With her foot, she edged it open the rest of the way.

Cedar-lined, the closet was as bare and empty as everything else. Yet her unease remained. Teri stared at the cedar paneling, fighting a mounting excitement.

She was on her knees running her fingers along the baseboard looking for a release when the dark space grew ominously darker. Teri spun, coming to her feet in a burst of adrenaline.

R.J. filled the entrance. His hair and clothing were damp, but it was the scowl on his face that set her stomach churning.

"You scared me!"

"What do you think you're doing?" he demanded roughly.

"Looking for a hidden room."

"There isn't one in there."

"How do you know?"

He turned without answering. Teri followed him into Valerie's bedroom, relieved to be out of the confined space, especially given R.J.'s apparent mood. What had Lester said to him?

"The opening to the hidden passage is out here," he told her flatly, indicating the wall next to the bathroom entrance.

"There is one?"

"Check it out. You'll find it's still sealed shut from the other side. Wyatt checked all this after Valerie disappeared. This passage connects with the attic and the room next door, but neither entrance has been tampered with since I sealed them."

His steely gaze watched as she tried to move the hidden lever and couldn't. She faced him uncertainly. Tiredly, he rubbed at his jaw.

"I thought Wyatt had this room locked up."

"He did. I sort of borrowed the master key," she told him.

His features tightened as he took it from her fingers without touching her.

"Ian thought someone was in here earlier. I thought I should check it out."

He stared at her in silence for a long moment.

"Who is Olivia?"

Teri stared mutely at the intractable expression on his face.

"Sorry," he said, looking angry rather than sorry. "Wrong question. I should have asked what is Olivia's relationship to Valerie?"

Cold washed over her. What *had* Lester said to him outside? Whatever it was, R.J. had obviously bought into the lie.

"Lester isn't what he appears to be, R.J. I told you that."

"You haven't told me anything."

Anger made him seem larger. She quailed inside but refused to back away. His gaze swept the room.

"What is that?"

"What is what?" But she was already bending down to pull on what turned out to be the ear of a stuffed toy dog. The tip of ear had been protruding from under the bed. She held the soft toy, hoping he didn't notice her hands had started shaking.

"Corey's?" she asked.

R.J. nodded. "He was holding it the last time I saw him. I thought Wyatt had this room cleared out. He must have missed that."

"Tell me where he is. Please, R.J. If I don't get to Corey before Lester does, he'll take the boy and disappear."

"Why would he do that? He seemed very worried about his wife."

"Of course he is," she agreed scathingly. "If Valerie is able to come forward and talk to the police, she'll make things difficult for him. You saw her, R.J. You know what he did to her."

Teri realized she was crushing the toy against her chest, but she didn't let it go.

"I don't know that Boyington did anything to her," R.J. said slowly. "Are you aware that she'd made friends with a young man whose parents own the farm next to their place? The man had several arrests for possession of narcotics. He also disappeared shortly before Valerie did."

His words shocked her, but she cast them aside. "I told you not to trust anything Lester says."

"*Wyatt* told me this the other night. He got the information from the chief of police in Maryland."

Her stomach clenched.

"As an investigator, aren't you supposed to be keeping an open mind, Teri? The man's own parents admit their son has a temper. Valerie never told me who beat her. I made the assumption it was her husband, but the fact is, she refused to press charges against him. We argued about it the evening she disappeared. At the time, it didn't occur to me that she might have a very good reason for refusing to press charges against her husband."

"Of course she had a reason! It's called fear. She knew he'd kill her."

"Or Boyington wasn't the one who hit her."

"You really believe that?" Teri felt her fear and frustration mounting. Lester had charmed him just as she'd feared.

"You have to see how well it all fits. If she had an addiction problem…"

"If!"

"…and she hooked up with a man who could help supply her, a man with known connections and a quick temper…" He shrugged. "They argue, he beats her and she takes off because she knows her husband will put her in treatment, maybe even divorce her."

"She should be so lucky!"

He ignored the interruption, his words spilling like pebbles against her skin.

"So she contacts me, gets me to help her. Who knows, maybe she even planned to seek help for her addiction, only I pressed her to file a complaint too hard. She was scared."

"At least you got that part right."

He ignored her pointed words.

"She calls this guy and arranges for him to come and get her, knowing if she leaves Corey here he'll be taken care of."

Teri clenched her fists until her fingernails bit into her skin. "You have it all figured out, don't you?"

Abruptly, R.J. closed his eyes. His tight expression faded.

"I don't have anything figured out, Teri. I have a hypothesis that fits. And instead of blindly assuming anything, *I'm* trying to keep an open mind."

"So, after this so-called drug abuser beat her badly enough that she took sanctuary here, she abandoned Corey to go back to him so he could do it all over again."

A muscle twitched in his jaw. "Maybe. If she needed drugs that badly," he agreed. "Or maybe she ran away after she got here because she believed he'd followed her here. No," he corrected immediately, "she wouldn't have left her son."

"Corey isn't her son."

Too late to bite back the words, she cursed herself for a fool.

"What did you say?"

There was no taking it back. Nothing for it but to tell him the rest.

"Lester was married before."

R.J. blinked, absorbing her words. "Okay, all the more reason to believe she ran off with this neighbor and left Corey behind."

"You don't get it, do you? Lester made that story up about her using drugs."

"You don't know that."

"I know it makes a perfect cover story." She held his gaze, willing him to believe her. "If you're keeping an open mind, then think about this. What better way to control his women than to keep them isolated by spreading vicious rumors guaranteed to keep other people away."

"His women?"

"Lester abused his first wife, too. He moved Rosalynn away from everyone she knew. Then he spread lies about her mental stability to keep her from making new friends. Do you see a pattern here?"

Her voice shook. She took a deep breath to steady herself.

"Like Valerie, Rosalynn was young and on her own. By the time she saw through Lester's charm and realized what was happening, it was too late. She told herself all the usual things. He didn't mean to hit her. He only did it because she said the wrong thing, or because he was drunk, or angry about something else." She shut her eyes for a moment opening them to find him watching her intently. "Once he'd eroded her confidence, it was easy. She didn't know how to escape."

"How do you know this?"

Squeezing the stuffed dog tightly, she tried to keep her features impassive. She was already regretting her impassioned words, but she reminded herself that she needed R.J.'s help.

"Rosalynn was supposed to have been one of the victims in those floods down in Texas several months ago."

Something dark flickered across his face.

"Several bodies were never recovered," she continued, trying to drive home her point. "The authorities believe they were washed into the Gulf or buried under tons of silt and mud and debris. They say the bodies will turn up eventually. Hers won't."

"What are you saying?"

"I'm saying that Lester Boyington is not what he appears to be. A flood makes a real convenient way to dispose of an unwanted body or two."

She held up her hand to stave off his protest. "You met him, R.J. Would you say Lester struck you as the type of man to marry three months after his wife disappeared in a flood? Because that's exactly what he did. Three months isn't much time to mourn the mother of his child, is it? Nor much time to woo and court a new bride—unless he'd already been doing so before his wife vanished. And hey! Now wife number two has disappeared, as well. No major flood this time, but again, no body, either."

"Are you implying Boyington killed his first wife?"

"Lester travels all the time, R.J. It shouldn't be too hard to prove he'd been spending time wherever Valerie was living before his first wife died. Someone must know when she started dating him."

"Shouldn't you have investigated this already?"

She nodded. "I would have if I'd had time. I didn't. I was trying to get to them before anyone else got hurt."

His eyes clouded as he digested her words. "You do realize you're suggesting that Boyington is a serial killer."

"I'm telling you he's a ruthless man who likes to

control women and gets his kicks out of hurting them. I think when someone takes the time to dig into his past, they're going to find a real scary pattern of behavior there."

R.J. rubbed his jaw. The tired gesture said a lot about the turmoil going on inside his head.

"You think Valerie is dead. That he killed her."

"I'm sorry, R.J., but yeah. I do. I think he lured her outside with a phone call and made sure she wouldn't be filing any police reports."

R.J. swore under his breath.

"I knew you wouldn't believe me."

"I didn't say I didn't believe you," he said angrily. "Give me some proof."

She thought about her sister lying in that sterile hospital bed unable to tell anyone anything. She'd be helpless if Lester found out where she was.

Seeing Lester again had sparked the soul-deep fear inside Teri. It was that fear, coupled with what she knew about Lester's ability to sway people, that had kept her from going to the authorities in the first place. When it came down to a "he said, she said" sort of accusation, there was no doubt in Teri's mind which of them would win.

"I don't have any proof."

"And I can't let you kidnap Corey."

"Valerie did that! All I want to do is take him out of Lester's reach."

"Lester is his father. He's got rights, Teri."

"I don't care! What about Corey's rights? What about the rights of his mother?"

"Who is Olivia?"

The question stopped her.

"Who, Teri? Grandmother? Aunt? Who?"

The stubborn set of his jaw told her that he wasn't going to budge on this issue, but it didn't matter anymore.

"Olivia is Rosalynn's aunt."

R.J. rocked back on his heels. "Will she confirm your story about Lester?"

Defeated, she lowered her gaze. "Olivia never met him."

He straightened abruptly. "We need to take this to Wyatt."

"Why? There's nothing he can do. His hands are tied."

"So are mine, Teri."

She made one last desperate attempt. "Don't you get it? Once Lester has Corey, he's out of here. He'll disappear again and all the proof in the world won't protect that little boy! Please, you have to tell me where Corey is!"

She knew by his posture what his answer would be before he spoke.

"I can't do that."

"You mean you won't."

His sigh was deep, his expression troubled. "Look at it from my point of view."

"I don't have time for your point of view! If you won't help me I'll find another way."

"I can't let you do that, Teri. Wyatt—"

"I am sick to death of hearing about your invisible friend Wyatt." Anger vibrated through her. "He's a cop. He has to play by the rules. Men like Lester don't believe in rules. They're predators. I don't have the luxury of time right now to prove what I'm telling you. But whatever you believe, R.J., I promise you this, Lester Boyington is the most dangerous man you'll ever meet."

Clutching the stuffed toy, she pushed past him without another word.

Chapter Eleven

His hand nearly reached out to stop her, but at the last second R.J. let her go. They both needed a few minutes to calm down. Except calm wasn't something he could manage at the moment. Teri had led him to believe she was there to help Valerie when all along her goal had been to kidnap Corey.

The sting of her deception was surprisingly painful. He'd come to trust her. He'd *wanted* to trust her. Why hadn't she told him the truth from the start?

Come to that, was she telling him the truth now?

Confronting her again wouldn't change anything. Instead, he pulled out his phone and dialed Wyatt's cell phone. The call immediately went to voice mail. Disconnecting, he tried the Crossley house.

Alexis answered after several rings. R.J. strove to keep his voice from betraying his emotions.

"Hey there, am I getting you from something?"

"Changing a diaper."

"Okay. Yuck. And congratulations. Are you okay that it wasn't a girl like your sisters each had?"

"Of course I am." There was laughter in her voice. "Wyatt and I were hoping for a boy, and he's gorgeous, R.J.. He looks just like Wyatt."

"Sorry to hear that."

Her laughter came again. "Now you're in trouble. I think he heard that. He's standing right here reaching for the phone. Come on over and meet the newest Crossley when you get a chance."

"But not right away," Wyatt's masculine voice said in his ear, obviously having taken the phone from his wife. "This had better be important, R.J."

His tension returned. "It is. Lester Boyington arrived looking for Corey."

Wyatt listened without interruption as R.J. gave him an abbreviated version of the situation, including what they had discovered in the basement and in the library.

"With the gate down, we're sitting here wide-open right now."

Wyatt swore. "I don't have the manpower to send someone out there to stand guard, R.J. I'll deal with Jacob later, and I'll call the station and let them know to stall Boyington until we can run a more thorough check on him. And speaking of checks, there's no record of a private investigator from Texas by the name of Teri Johnson."

"She's not licensed?"

"As far as we can determine, she doesn't exist. There's no agency, no print ads, nothing. And that car she's driving? It's registered to an Olivia Barnesly."

"The aunt."

"Maybe. If Teri told you the truth."

R.J. gripped his phone more tightly. "Could she be licensed somewhere else? She doesn't have a Texan accent."

"I'll start people checking on that, also on Olivia Barnesly and prior marriages for Boyington. What did you say the name of the first wife was?"

"Teri only referred to her as Rosalynn. She implied Boyington moved to Texas from somewhere else."

"Corey's birth certificate should give us more information," he muttered, more to himself than to R.J. "I need to talk to this Teri."

"That's what I figured."

"Under no circumstances take her to George and Emily's."

"Wasn't planning to," R.J. agreed mildly.

"Sorry."

"What about Boyington?" R.J. asked.

"No one is getting near that kid until I have a few answers. I'll let George and Emily know."

"You don't think they're in any danger, do you?"

Wyatt hesitated. "No, but I'll alert George to take a few precautions."

"What do you want me to do?"

"Go through the house and board up all the passages again. Especially that entrance through the library. I want you to go over Heartskeep from top to bottom. I've had my fill of secret rooms and passages. If there's so much as a mouse hole, I want it plugged."

"What about Teri? You want me to keep her here?"

"You don't have that kind of authority, R.J. I'll handle it. I should be there inside an hour."

"Sorry. I didn't mean to pull you away from your family."

"Part of the job. I'll see you in an hour."

Only after he disconnected did R.J. remember that he hadn't told Wyatt that Teri was armed.

IAN WATCHED HIS MOM pick at her food without eating. He could almost taste her fear. He'd thought maybe she was scared because the gate had been destroyed, but when he'd tried to ask her she'd patted him on the shoulder and told him not to worry.

He hated being a kid.

He stared at his plate, no longer interested in the macaroni and cheese, even though it was one of his favorites. The helpless feeling swelled in his chest until he thought he'd burst from the pressure. If only he was bigger. If only he could make things right.

Abruptly, his mother told him to finish his lunch and excused herself, saying she wasn't feeling well and she was going upstairs to lie down. Ian sat there as long as he could, but the sliding, sympathetic glances everyone was sending him when they thought he wouldn't notice made him even angrier.

With a clatter, he dropped his fork on his plate and stood so fast his chair tipped over.

"Sorry," he mumbled. "I have to check on my mom."

"Ian! Wait."

He scooted across the room before Mrs. Walsh or anyone else could stop him.

He knew they meant well. He even sort of liked it here, though Heartskeep was kind of scary. Nola and Boone were pretty cool for little kids and they understood how he felt. He didn't want to run again. Where would they go?

They couldn't go home. His mom had called their next-door neighbor yesterday and she'd said *he* was still at the house. It wasn't fair. It was *their* house.

Ian missed his room and his things and his friends. And his mom missed their cat, Kittina. *He'd* thrown her cat outside that night and threatened to kill her. That's why his mother had called Mrs. Sandler yesterday. She'd told his mom she'd seen Kittina and promised to take her in and feed her until they could go back for her.

But they'd never be able to go back as long as *he* was still there. Ian knew it was evil, but he wished *he'd* die of some horrible disease or get hit by a car or something. Anything so they could have their old lives back.

He paused outside the door to their room, not sure what to say to his mom. He heard her moving around inside and paused to listen. The sound of a suitcase being unzipped froze his hand on the door. The dresser drawer opened next. His stomach tightened. He'd been right. They were leaving.

His eyes burned with unshed tears as he turned away and ran to the far end of the hall. It wasn't fair. If only his dad hadn't died. His dad wouldn't have let Russell Eastman hurt his mother. But if his dad hadn't died, she never would have married *him*.

Why did his dad have to go and die, anyhow? Didn't he know Ian was too little to protect his mother? He was doing the best he could, but it wasn't enough!

He pressed his forehead against the large glass picture window and tried not to cry, even though his eyes burned and his throat was all thick and hurting with need.

He hated *him*. He wished he was bigger. He wished—

Ian blinked back the unshed tears as his gaze was drawn to something moving in the trees that lined the driveway. He watched intently as a figure hurried toward the house. For a split second, a man's blond head and face came into view as the person stopped to stare up at the house.

The hollow, scared feeling inside Ian intensified as he stared at that face. The instant the man ducked behind another tree, Ian whirled. Quaking with fear, he ran to warn his mother. It was too late for them to go anywhere.

He was already here.

TERI TUCKED THE GUN into her jacket pocket and surveyed the room. She hadn't unpacked anything, so she was ready to go. She tried to ignore the nagging inner voice that said leaving was a bad idea. She had to find Corey and head back to Texas.

Picking up the stuffed dog, she hugged it to her chest, picturing Corey as she'd seen him last. He was such a sweet little boy. She had to find him.

While Lester wouldn't go out of his way to physically harm Corey, he'd do whatever he had to do to protect himself. And if that meant killing his only child, Teri knew he'd do it in a heartbeat.

Even without physically abusing Corey, Lester could do a lot of psychological damage in a short amount of time. Teri's only chance was to find Corey first—an almost impossible task without R.J.'s help.

"Going somewhere?"

R.J. filled the open doorway. Anger still simmered in his accusing eyes.

"Yes."

"Want to explain why the police can't find any record of a private investigator by the name of Teri Johnson in Texas?"

His tone stiffened her spine. "No."

"Who are you, Teri? Your car's registered to Olivia Barnesly."

She'd known the police would discover that the minute an investigation was launched. She mustn't panic.

"Will the police turn Corey over to Lester right away?"

A muscle near his jaw twitched in agitation. "No."

She still had time, then.

"Is Olivia Barnesly really Corey's aunt?"

"Great-aunt," she corrected.

"And she's your client?"

Teri squeezed the stuffed dog. Something inside crinkled. Glancing down, she frowned and squeezed harder. R.J. said something else, but she was no longer listening. Studying the dog, she discovered a carefully repaired tear in the side seam of the fluffy toy.

"What are you doing?" R.J. demanded.

Teri kneaded the stuffed toy in mounting excitement. "It can't be."

"What can't be?"

She didn't spare him a glance as her fingernails tugged at the thread that closed the seam.

"This is so Hollywood cliché."

He clamped his jaw shut on another question and watched her. His anger faded to puzzlement as she worked the seam.

"I need a pair of scissors."

"Will this do?"

He handed her a small pocketknife with several tools.

"Where do you hide something you don't want your husband to find?" she asked as she worked to rip out the seam.

"What are you talking about?"

"I think Valerie left us a clue."

His gaze went from her to the dog. "You're right. That is a Hollywood cliché."

Opening the threads, she inserted two fingers deep into the stuffing.

"Uh-huh. Maybe that's why it's effective. There's something in here. It feels like a sheet of paper."

R.J. held the toy so she could work the paper out with two fingers. Neither said a word as she unfolded the plain white sheet.

"What is it?"

Six names formed a column, written in a familiar tight script. The first two names had been crossed off. They meant nothing to her, but with a sickening feeling of dread Teri recognized the third name down. She raised her gaze to R.J., ignoring the betraying shake of her fingers.

"Cassandra Downing and her husband were killed in a home invasion in Virginia less than a week ago. It was all over the news because they were prominent attorneys. The police have no suspects. What do you want to bet the first two names that are crossed off are also dead?"

"Let me see that."

R.J. took the paper and studied the names.

"Bennett Winslow was killed in a carjacking in D.C. a little over a week ago," he said.

"The first name on the list?"

"Uh-huh. And this fourth name, Joshua Fromm? If I'm not mistaken, he's the guy who was shot and killed in a robbery attempt in that parking garage in D.C. two days ago."

Their gazes locked. His expression was shaken.

"I could be wrong."

"You know you're not." She felt so cold she wondered if she'd ever be warm again. "Looks like when you called Lester a serial killer, you weren't far off the mark. He's a professional hit man."

R.J. shook his head in flat denial.

"You're jumping to conclusions."

"Given this list, how would you jump?"

"It could mean anything," he protested.

"Right. Lester just likes to compile the names of people who are going to die violently."

"We don't know that Boyington has anything to do with this list."

"That's his handwriting."

His eyes narrowed. "How do you know?"

"I know what his handwriting looks like."

R.J. stared hard at her for several long minutes. Then he reached for his cell phone.

"Who are you calling?"

"Wyatt. You're sure about the handwriting?"

"Positive. R.J., we can't wait for your friend. We have to get Corey away from here!"

He spoke into the phone as someone answered. "Alexis, let me talk to Wyatt... He did? How long ago?... Okay, thanks, Alexis, I'll try that.... No. Everything's fine.... Really? I'll have to work on my voice control." His lighter tone was not reflected on his features. "I have some additional information for him. Look, I have to go. The battery on my phone is dying. Wyatt can explain everything to you later."

He disconnected and grimaced. Shoving his phone back in its holder, he rubbed his jaw wearily.

"Alexis can pick the worst time to turn into a mind reader. Wyatt's on his way."

He crossed to the telephone beside her bed and began pushing buttons.

"Who are you calling now?"

"His cell phone."

"R.J., we don't have time for this!"

Abruptly, his features hardened.

"You may be right," he said as he set the phone back in the handset.

"What's wrong?"

"The phone's dead."

"Is it plugged in?"

He looked down. His expression was all the answer she needed.

"Maybe the rain…?"

But even as she glanced toward the smeared window-panes, she knew the phone wasn't out because of the rain.

"He's here, isn't he?" He'd recognized her after all.

"Why would he come back?"

"Because he didn't believe you when you told him Corey wasn't here?" She prayed that was the reason.

"Have you got your gun?"

She nodded, not trusting her voice.

"On you?"

She patted her jacket pocket. R.J. headed for the hall. "We need to let the others know, but let's try not to start a panic."

Too late. Her insides were roiling in panic. Lester was coming for her.

Together they left the room. Betty Drexler was just coming out of the Sutter's bedroom across the hall. She waved and hurried toward them. R.J. swore softly under his breath. Teri knew how he felt.

At least four of the names on that list were dead. Lester was ruthless enough to kill everyone in Hearts-keep if he felt it was necessary. But surely with this many people inside, even he wouldn't take that sort of chance.

Would he?

No! If he'd recognized her, she had to believe he'd try to catch her alone. And to do that, he would need to find a way inside.

Unless he was already in the house.

Betty Drexler rushed up to them.

"R.J.! Have you or Teri seen Evelyn or Ian?"

"No."

Her frightened expression stopped them both.

"They're gone!"

"What do you mean, gone?" he demanded.

"Evelyn wasn't feeling well at lunch. She came up to lie down and Ian followed her. I just checked on them. Their room is empty."

"It's a big house, Betty. Maybe they're in the library," R.J. began brusquely.

"No. You don't understand. Everything's gone. Their suitcases...everything." Her lower lip trembled. "She was scared. I could see something was bothering her, but I didn't have a chance to talk to her. It must have had something to do with that phone call."

I'm afraid I've done something extraordinarily foolish, she'd told Teri.

"What phone call?" R.J. demanded.

"She called her neighbor yesterday to see if the woman would take care of her cat."

Teri felt a flash of fear. "Did she use her cell phone?"

"No. She used the house phone. Why?"

"Because if the neighbor has caller ID, it's possible her husband knows where she is."

Teri and R.J. exchanged speaking looks. What if it hadn't been Lester who had cut the phone line?

"Where are your kids, Betty?"

"In the playroom. Is something wrong?"

"No," Teri said.

"Yes," R.J. replied at the same time.

Betty looked from one to the other, a wild fear growing in her expression.

"Go stay with your kids, Betty," R.J. told her. "Keep them in the playroom, all right?"

Her features blanched. "What's wrong?"

"Maybe nothing. Do you know where everyone else is?"

"Mrs. Norwhich is in the kitchen. I think the others are in the living room watching a soap opera. What's wrong, R.J.?"

"We aren't sure yet," he admitted, "but there may be an intruder on the grounds. Stay with your kids until we know it's safe."

Betty started to ask another question but bit it off, whirled around and scurried away.

"I thought you didn't want to start a panic."

"She was already scared," R.J. pointed out.

They plunged down the back stairs. Mrs. Norwhich looked up from the sink where she was chopping vegetables.

"Is the house alarm on?" R.J. demanded.

"No. Will turned it off a little while ago."

"Turn it on!" Teri demanded.

"It won't do any good," R.J. pointed out. "The alarm is tied to the phone line. With the phone line dead, the alarm system can't dial out for help."

"But it will still sound the alarm, won't it?"

"Yeah."

Mrs. Norwhich didn't wait for explanations. She hustled to the alarm and switched it on.

Teri shook her head. "More than likely, it's already too late. He's probably already inside."

The older woman brandished the large knife she'd been using. "Who is?"

"Lester Boyington."

"Or Evelyn's husband," R.J. pointed out.

"Do you know which car belongs to Evelyn Sutter?" Teri asked.

"That black Mercedes."

They looked to where she pointed with the knife. The car didn't appear disturbed. It could have been sitting there forever.

"Did Evelyn take anything out to her car today?" R.J. asked.

"No. I'd have seen her if she had. I haven't left this kitchen all day."

"Is Kathy in the living room, too?"

"As far as I know."

"What about Will?" R.J. asked.

"He's in the basement. I think he went to meet Jacob."

"Jacob is here?"

Her bony shoulders rose and fell. "He didn't come in through the kitchen if he is. Will talked to him on the phone right after lunch. Then he told Kathy he'd be in the basement if anyone needed him."

R.J. and Teri exchanged glances.

"Wyatt's on his way," R.J. told the woman. "I think it might be a good idea to get everyone together in one room until he gets here."

"What about Evelyn and Ian?" Teri asked.

"We'll get Will and do a room-by-room search."

"What should I tell everyone?" Mrs. Norwhich demanded.

"The truth," R.J. advised. "Tell them we think there's a prowler. The police are on the way and we're locking down the house until they get here. Have Kathy gather everyone in the playroom. Tell her to hurry. I'll get Will."

As R.J. headed for the basement, Mrs. Norwhich

wiped her hands, picked up the large knife again and left the kitchen.

Teri fingered her gun. Staring nervously out at the bleak landscape she scanned the area for any sign of movement as the seconds ticked past. Lester was a consummate actor, but there hadn't been a flicker of recognition when he'd looked at her earlier. Had he recognized her?

And then it came to her that her aunt's car with its Texas plates was sitting out front in plain sight. If he'd been paying any attention at all, he wouldn't have missed that.

She winced. Texas was a huge state, but Lester was far from stupid. He'd know their bodies had never been recovered. And Heartskeep was where Valerie had taken his son. The minute he saw a Texas plate, he'd probably decided she and her sister were here.

What was taking R.J. and Will so long?

Teri crossed to the basement door. R.J. had left it ajar. She reached for the handle. Coldness surrounded her. The door swung shut without making a sound.

Every hair on her body stood at attention. Was every door in this house haunted? Teri forced her shaky hand to touch the doorknob. It wouldn't turn, as if someone stood on the other side holding the knob.

Adrenaline fed her sense of urgency. Whirling, she ran to the spare bedroom. Her senses were screaming that R.J. was in trouble or he would have been back upstairs by now.

The hidden panel opened without trouble. The darkness inside nearly held her at bay, but there wasn't time to go for a flashlight. The tiny flash on her key chain would have to serve. Its light was enough to help her open the second panel to the stairs.

Tiny skittering sounds below added to her jumpy nerves. The thought of rodents hiding in the dark watching her made her shudder. She reached the bottom and debated whether to call out.

An explosion of gunshots rang out in answer to her thought. The sound echoed off the cinder blocks and concrete, only slightly louder than the sound made by the old elevator as it suddenly clanked and groaned to life.

Chapter Twelve

Teri heard the whine of bullets striking metal and realized the person was shooting at the elevator. She switched off her light and flew back up the steps. R.J. did not have a gun. There was no reason to believe Will did, either, so the shooter wasn't them. If R.J. and Will were inside the elevator, they wouldn't be able to get out!

She thrust her gun into her pocket and tried to think. Her only tool was the screwdriver she'd taken from Jacob's toolbox. She pulled it from her pocket. She'd need more than this to pull down those heavy walls.

Last night, the men had said something about dead space between the library and the bathroom. Why hadn't she paid more attention? Solid wood walls stretched forever, broken only by the five doorways. How could she possibly know where to start looking for them?

Dismayed, she shot a worried glance toward the basement door. Was the door still locked? He'd be coming up here any minute now otherwise.

Teri pounded on the wall outside the library. "R.J.! Can you hear me? R.J.?"

There was no sound. She couldn't hear the elevator

anymore, either. Had it stopped between floors or gone on to the second floor? Even if it were stopped right in front of her, R.J. probably wouldn't hear her through the thick wood paneling.

A sound from inside the library sent her spinning toward the double doors. Jacob peered around the corner.

"You!"

He eyed the screwdriver she held like a weapon and stepped into the hall. He was holding a sheaf of papers.

"What's going on? What's with the screwdriver?"

"I need your help!"

Bemused, he shook his head. "I can honestly say I didn't expect that sort of a greeting from you."

"R.J. and Will are trapped in the elevator. We have to get them out."

"They're inside the elevator?"

She shot another glance down the hall. "There's someone in the basement with a gun. I'm guessing they used the elevator to escape when he started shooting."

"Whoa! Someone's in the basement shooting at them?"

"Yes! We have got to get them out!"

He shook his head. "I was just down there with Will. I had to run back to my car to get these papers, but there was no one down there then."

"Well, there is now!"

"Okay. Okay! He's still down there?"

"Yes!" She struggled to gain control of the panic threatening to take over. "We have to get them out!" She wanted to rip the walls down with her bare hands. "They could be hurt. Wounded!"

"All right, take it easy. That screwdriver isn't going

to do us much good. We need real tools. Unfortunately, mine are in the basement."

Teri shoved the screwdriver into her pocket. "There must be something up here you can use!"

"Well, Kathy keeps a few tools in the laundry room."

"Let's go!"

"Where is everybody?" he asked, following her down the hall.

"We told Mrs. Norwhich to keep everyone together in the playroom. The police are on the way."

"Glad to hear that, at least."

As they neared the basement, Teri pulled out her gun. Jacob's eyes widened.

"What are you doing?"

"In case he comes up the stairs."

Jacob cursed. "You do know how to use that thing, right?"

"Point and squeeze. Go! Hurry!"

Teri stopped short of the basement door and waited. Jacob muttered but kept going.

She couldn't be sure the door was still locked. What she was sure of was the gunman would be coming up after R.J. and Will. She steeled herself to fire the moment the door began to open.

And then she remembered the hidden stairs. The cinder-block wall would have closed. If the shooter didn't know how to get it open again, he'd go exploring. She hadn't closed the openings at the top of the stairs!

An eerie coldness seemed to move through her as Teri had that thought. She pivoted as a tall shape rushed at her from the spare bedroom.

There wasn't time to scream. His blow glanced off her cheek, but the force of his charge caused her to fall heavily against the paneling. The stocky blond stranger wrenched the gun from her fingers and sent it spinning down the hall. Teri tried to struggle, but he grabbed her in a vise of steel and thrust her back against the wall.

Fear held her in place far more effectively than the forearm he used to pin her neck.

"Where's Evelyn? Where's my wife?"

Russell Eastman. The dark gleam in his eyes was terrifyingly similar to the look Lester turned on his prey.

"I don't know," she managed to gasp out.

He shoved the barrel of a gun against her temple.

"I'm only going to ask you one more time. Where is she?"

The stale smell of onions on his breath made her want to gag. But it was his savage look of pleasure that riveted her attention. He was enjoying her fear.

And in that second, fear turned to fury. She would not be a victim again. Her fingers slid to her pocket as she stalled for time.

"I sent them out back. To the barns. I was just checking the house, making sure everyone was out."

He lowered his weapon and wrenched her around toward the kitchen.

"Show me."

As he gave her a shove, she pulled the screwdriver from her pocket. Pivoting, she drove it under his coat and into his side as hard as she could. He screamed, high and shrill in shocked surprise, but he didn't let her go. Instead, he brought the butt of the gun down against her head.

Pain exploded. It sounded like a gunshot. A detached part of her watched a chip of wood fly past her cheek as he slammed her against the wall. Her release was so abrupt she slid down the paneling to the floor.

Through blurred vision Teri glimpsed Ian and Evelyn near the dining room entrance. Evelyn was taking Teri's gun from Ian. The sound she'd heard had been one of them firing the weapon.

Russell lurched in their direction with a snarl of satisfaction.

"No!" Ian shouted, running forward. "I won't let you hurt my mother again!"

The man backhanded Ian with such force the boy crumpled to the floor like a broken toy. Evelyn brought up the muzzle of Teri's gun.

"What are you going to do, Evelyn? Shoot me?" Russell sneered.

He laughed, a harsh grating sound. And as he continued moving toward her, he brought up his own gun.

From behind them, Jacob shouted, "Hey!"

Ian started scrambling to his feet. Teri grabbed him, yanking him down just in time. Russell spun and fired. The sound was deafening. Jacob fell to the floor.

As Russell turned back in her direction, the gun in Evelyn's hand spat a flash of flame. Russell staggered. He fired in return, but Teri could see the shot would go wild. Evelyn didn't move as he continued lurching toward her. With hate in her eyes, she squeezed the trigger over and over until the gun clicked on an empty chamber. Russell said something and collapsed at her feet.

With the metallic scent of cordite and blood filling her head, Teri released Ian and scrabbled across the floor to where Russell's hand still gripped his gun. Jerking it free, she saw he was still alive. He mouthed an expletive at her, but his angry eyes were clouding with shock. Unable to look away, she watched them glaze and close.

"Is he dead?" Ian whispered.

Teri felt for a pulse. "No, he's alive. But he needs an ambulance."

Somehow, Teri got to her feet. Evelyn hadn't moved. She stared at her husband without expression. Shoving Russell's gun into her pocket, Teri took her own gun from Evelyn's unresisting fingers, shoving it into her waistband.

"You picked the perfect moment to find that back-bone," Teri told her softly.

Evelyn's gaze remained focused on her husband. "I had no choice. Ian picked up your gun. I couldn't let *him* shoot Russell. I didn't want to shoot him, either."

"I know. It will be okay, Evelyn. Ian, stay with your mom while I check on Jacob."

Jacob was on his feet, swaying slightly. Blood stained his shirt, seeping between the fingers clutching his left forearm.

"How bad are you hurt?" she asked.

"Not as bad as I would have been if he'd taken the time to aim," he told her with a grimace. "And wouldn't you know, it's the same damn arm."

There was no time to ask what he was talking about. The sound of running footsteps sent her reaching for Russell's gun as she whirled to face the new threat.

R.J. and Will charged out of the spare bedroom and came to a dead stop as they took in the chaos.

"Is everyone all right?" R.J. demanded.

Relieved past words, she lowered the gun. "Jacob took a bullet. Evelyn had to shoot Russell Eastman. He needs an ambulance right away."

Will pulled out a cell phone and began to punch in numbers.

"How did you get out of the elevator?"

"It goes to the attic," R.J. told her. "There's another hidden room up there, of course, but the elevator doors weren't boarded over. We used the hidden stairs to come back down."

"Russell used them, too. He probably couldn't get back through the cinder blocks." Teri wished she'd considered that possibility sooner.

"Are *you* all right?" R.J. demanded urgently.

"Fine, but Evelyn's in shock, and he hit Ian pretty hard. You'd better see how badly Jacob's hurt first."

Will was still speaking into the phone as he bent over Russell Eastman.

R.J. crossed to Jacob. The younger man offered him a weak smile.

"You'd think one of these days I'd learn it doesn't pay to rescue a damsel in distress. I always end up hurt, and someone else always ends up with the girl."

"Yeah. Thanks." R.J. tore open his shirt. "Teri, can you get me a clean towel from the kitchen? Looks like the bullet passed right through, Jacob. It's not too bad. I've seen worse on construction sites."

"Gee, that makes me feel so much better."

Teri tucked Eastman's gun back into her pocket and ran to the kitchen. Flinging open drawers, she found the dishtowels and scooped them up.

"You're lucky it was Eastman instead of Boyington," R.J. was telling Jacob when she returned. "At least Eastman isn't a professional killer. And it looks like he wasn't much of a shot, either."

Jacob paled. "The missing woman's husband is a professional killer?"

"We think so."

"I am definitely out of the rescue business, effective immediately."

"You make a habit of this?" Teri asked, feeling dizzy as she handed a towel to R.J. and took the rest to Will, who was trying to stanch the blood running from Russell Eastman's body.

"Only at Heartskeep," Jacob replied.

"Thanks," Will grunted. "Take one and apply pressure here. Wyatt should be arriving any second now, but this man is losing a lot of blood. He needs to be flown to a hospital immediately or he won't make it."

"Is he going to die?" Ian asked.

"I don't know, son. Why don't you go unlock the front door so Wyatt can get in?"

"The alarm's on," Teri warned.

"I'll get it," R.J. told her.

The hall filled with people shortly after that. Teri stayed with Will, keeping pressure on one wound while he did the same to another. She only glanced up once when she heard an unfamiliar masculine voice, but she relaxed as she recognized a police uniform. Wyatt Crossley had finally arrived.

"Where are the guns?" he asked.

"I have them," she said without looking at him. "Russell's gun is in my pocket. Mine is empty. It's tucked in my waistband."

"I'll get them," R.J. said.

"Be careful. The one in my pocket is still loaded."

His hand slid under her shirt, warm against her cold skin. He removed her gun first, then the other one, and handed them both to Wyatt.

"I saw him in the trees coming up the driveway," Ian was telling the chief. "I made my mom go down the hidden stairs into the secret room so he wouldn't find us. We didn't think he'd hurt anyone else."

"You did the right thing," Wyatt told him.

"Mom wanted to warn Mrs. Walsh, but Teri and R.J. were in the kitchen telling Mrs. Norwhich that the phone line had been cut. I was afraid, so I told Mom they already knew and made her stay hidden."

Ian sounded close to tears.

"It's okay," R.J. told him. "You had to protect your mother. You're going to have quite a shiner there, young man."

"I am?" he sounded almost pleased by the unexpected badge of his courage.

"Why would he cut the phone line?" someone asked. "Everyone has cell phones."

"Cutting the phone line kills the security system," Wyatt answered.

"Even so, it should have beeped to alert us when he opened a window," Mrs. Norwhich protested.

"I don't think he did," R.J. told her. "I think he saw Jacob leave and used the hidden entrance in the library."

"You mean it's my fault?" Jacob swore, then apologized. "I didn't see anyone."

"That probably saved your life, Jacob," R.J. told him. "More than likely, Eastman would have shot you if you'd spotted him. He was coming inside, one way or another."

"But how'd you and Will end up in the elevator?" Jacob asked.

"What elevator?" Mrs. Norwhich asked.

"It runs through the library and the front bedroom above it," R.J. explained. "Eastman caught us by surprise. Will was checking out the elevator when I went down to get him."

"That's my fault, too. I called him on my way back here this morning and told him about it," Jacob admitted. "I thought maybe he'd have some idea how we could incorporate it into our plan."

"You were supposed to hang around last night," R.J. accused.

"I know, but I remembered I had a new client meeting this morning. I had to drive clear to he…heck," he amended with a glance at the children and shrugged apologetically. "You wouldn't believe the route I had to take to get back to New York last night so I could make the meeting. Then I had to do it again to come back here. You'd already gone to bed when I remembered, and I didn't want to wake you."

Teri glanced up. R.J. gave the younger man a dark look. Jacob shrugged and winced. "You still didn't say how you ended up in the elevator."

"Eastman followed me down. I didn't realize it until he came out of the shadows holding a gun. Will tossed a wrench at him, and we both darted inside the elevator and closed the door. I didn't expect Will to start the thing up."

"No choice," Will said mildly. "He started shooting. And that helicopter better hurry."

"It's on the way," Wyatt assured him.

"You're lucky you didn't get stuck in there," Jacob said.

"Yeah. It gave us a few bad moments. I had visions of being trapped inside the walls with no one knowing we were there. Fortunately, it took us straight to the attic."

"Good thing those cables held," Jacob said.

"Hey! There are some people running up the driveway," someone yelled. "I think they're paramedics."

Not until the newcomers ordered her to move did Teri surrender her position and stand. She swayed as everything grayed at the edges. No one seemed to notice and since her vision cleared after a second she didn't say anything.

"Are you all right?" R.J. asked, moving to her side.

Okay, so maybe he'd noticed. "Fine."

"You have blood all over."

"Big surprise. I'm not sure he's going to make it," she told him quietly.

"No, I mean, you're bleeding."

"I am?"

"Down the side of your head."

She raised a hand already sticky with blood, but R.J. stopped her.

"What's wrong?" Wyatt asked striding over.

"Teri's hurt."

"It's okay," she protested. But now that she was aware of the cut, her head began to throb and the room began to gray again. "He hit me with his gun. Guess it split the skin. I need…to wash…my hands."

"Grab her, R.J.!"

She tried to say she was fine, but R.J. caught her as her knees began to buckle and the hall grayed to black.

TERI PULLED her turtleneck back over her head carefully. Her head hurt like the devil, and several spectacular bruises were starting to form on various places on her body. Fortunately, most of them would be hidden by her clothing. But she didn't care. Either way, she was leaving this hospital right now if she had to walk all the way back to Heartskeep to get her car. Where had R.J. gone?

She hadn't wanted to come here in the first place. And if it hadn't meant avoiding a protracted conversation with Wyatt Crossley, she probably wouldn't have allowed the second set of paramedics to drag her here. She had not needed a three-hour wait for some young kid fresh out of medical school to tell her she had a mild concussion.

At least she'd insisted R.J. bring her bag to the hospital. Unfortunately, it was sitting on the floor. She was pretty sure if she tried to bend over to pick it up, she'd join it down there.

Maybe if she squatted instead of bending...

"Are you supposed to be out of bed?" R.J. demanded, shoving aside the curtain.

"Yes!" She glared at him, defying him to correct her. "I'm leaving."

"Long walk to Heartskeep," he said mildly, a flicker of amusement in his eyes.

"Cute. You're real cute, you know that?"

"So they tell me."

"If you're done flirting with all the nurses, would you grab my bag and—"

"All set, Ms. Johnson?" the perky young woman in white asked. "We just need you to sign these forms. Now I know the doctor went over everything with you, but the instructions are printed on this sheet of paper here. Will you be supervising her care?" she asked R.J. with a smile that revealed two deep dimples.

"Yes."

"No," Teri said at the same time.

The dimples faded.

"I do not need a supervisor."

"Now, Ms. Johnson, head injuries are nothing to fool around with."

"I have no intention of fooling around with anything." She scrawled her name illegibly and thrust the clipboard back at the woman. "I'm leaving."

"Don't worry," R.J. soothed. "I spoke with the doctor. I'll watch her. She's really a very nice person under normal circumstances."

"No, I'm not." She gave R.J. a poisonous glare and started past him.

Her exit would have been better if she'd been able to stride away instead of taking small, careful steps. But her head felt like spun glass, with broken shards inside jabbing at her brain. She suspected the slightest breeze would take her down.

"That was rude," R.J. said as he came abreast of her at the doors.

"So was a three-hour wait to tell me what I already knew."

"Three and a half hours," he amended, far too cheerfully for her frame of mind.

The temperature outside had dropped significantly. Teri sucked in a sharp breath as the cold air hit her face. Still, she was glad to be away from the disinfectant smell of the hospital.

R.J. regarded her steadily. "I hope you feel better than you look."

"No, but gee, thanks for making me feel even better."

"Sorry," he said without sounding contrite. "My truck's over this way. The air's feeling a bit raw, but at least it stopped raining."

He had to slow his pace to match hers.

"I'm the one who should apologize, R.J. I was acting like—"

"Hey. It's okay. I'm not fond of hospitals myself."

He unlocked the door and held it open. Teri gazed up at the seat and contemplated the amount of energy required to climb inside. She was pretty sure walking would be easier. Before she realized what he was going to do, R.J. had dropped her bag and lifted her as easily as one of his wall panels, settling her on the seat without jarring her.

"I could have managed," she protested weakly.

"No question. I just didn't want to be standing here come morning."

"Very funny."

He winked unrepentantly, shut the door and came around the truck. Tossing her bag in back, he slid effortlessly behind the wheel.

"Show-off."

"How *do* you feel?"

"Like someone slammed the butt of a gun upside my head after knocking me around."

"That good, huh?"

"Yeah. Did you manage to find out how Jacob is while you were waiting for me? They wouldn't tell me anything in there."

"The doctor released him a little bit ago. His girlfriend came and picked him up."

"Wait a minute! He gets shot, all I get is a concussion and they release him before me?"

"You should have tried charm instead of snarling at them."

"Fat lot of good that would have done *me.* I'm not a good-looking male."

"For which I am perfectly happy."

R.J. grinned. Teri settled more comfortably against the seat, letting some of the tension ease from her body.

"Did any of those flirtatious young nurses tell you how Russell Eastman is doing?"

His grin faded. "He's still in surgery."

"I don't know whether to hope he makes it, or hope he doesn't."

"Worried Evelyn won't be able to handle his death?"

"No, she's proved she's as tough as she has to be. Ian's the one I'm worried about. Wishing someone was dead is one thing. Having your mother kill the person in your defense is something else."

"She didn't fire just to defend him."

"I know, but he's a kid. Want to bet that's how he's thinking?"

"No bets."

"Where are we going?"

"The Inn. You'll like it. Wyatt had everyone moved there for the night. It's something of a gathering spot for locals and tourists. Great food, if you're hungry."

"I'm not."

"Kitchen's probably closed by now, anyhow. We're lucky. Normally it's hard to get a room there at this time of year because everyone's driving around looking at the leaves. But with so many of the roads flooded out around here, The Inn was able to accommodate everyone for the night."

Teri fell silent for several minutes, wondering how to broach a subject she wasn't sure she even wanted to speculate about.

"R.J., do you believe in ghosts?"

Startled, he glanced her way before turning his attention back to the empty, dark stretch of road.

"Is there a reason for that question?"

She started to shake her head, realized how much it would hurt and refrained.

"Just making conversation."

"Interesting choice of subject matter, but okay. I've

never given the matter much thought. Are you telling me you saw one?"

"No!" But remembering the icy cold that had warned her moments before Russell had struck, she couldn't help wondering if she'd felt one.

"All that talk of Ian's got to you, huh? Well," R.J. said more thoughtfully, "I do know a lot of people believe Heartskeep is haunted. Some bad things and some strange things have happened there over the years, and you do get some strange noises and feelings when you're there alone, but I've done a lot of work on the place and I've never seen a ghost."

"Ever have a door close in your face?"

He shot her another look and frowned. "Just that passage into the hidden basement. Why?"

She decided not to mention the corner bedroom or the basement door for fear he'd think she was crazy. "You don't think that's weird enough?"

"Heartskeep is weird in general, but if you really want an answer to whether Hearstkeep is haunted, ask Kathy. She grew up there. She and her mother worked for the Hart family most of her life."

Teri decided she would ask Kathy if the opportunity presented itself because something had been looking out for her inside that house. Or maybe that was her mind playing tricks on her because of the concussion.

"I think you'll like The Inn, at any rate," R.J. told her. "While it's as old as Heartskeep, there's never been so much as a rumor that it's haunted."

"Glad to hear it, but tonight I'm not sure I'd care, as long as it has a bed."

"Tired?"

"Exhausted," Teri replied.

"Yeah, me too. It's way past my bedtime."

"How's Lucky doing?"

R.J. smiled. "He's fine. I spoke with Doc while I was waiting for you. Doc offered to drop him off at my foster parents' place until I can pick him up. I gather, like you, he isn't fond of hospitals. I think he was driving Doc crazy."

"I'm glad he's okay."

"Lucky lives up to his name, all right. And speaking of luck, at the risk of getting my face slapped, would you mind if I keep your room key after we check in? According to the doctor, someone should check on you a couple of times during the night to be sure you don't slip into a coma."

Her pulse gave an unexpected leap.

"And did he tell you how to prevent that from happening?" she asked lightly.

His mouth twitched. "No, now that you mention it, he didn't."

Teri hesitated. "Wouldn't it be easier to simply share a room?"

R.J. stilled. The atmosphere in the secluded cab suddenly became far more intimate than it had been only a few seconds ago.

"It's not like we didn't do it last night," she added quickly.

"True, but I should tell you that The Inn mostly has full-size beds rather than queen or king. The rooms are fairly small."

She thought about that. Then she thought about sleeping alone. "You planning to sprawl or snore?"

His teeth flashed in another grin. "Nope."

"Then there's no problem, is there?"

"Not if you aren't worried I might try something."

"My head may be cracked, R.J., but I still know how to make a man sing soprano."

"I'll remember that."

"See that you do."

Chapter Thirteen

The room *was* small. Even though he'd warned her, R.J. could tell Teri hadn't been prepared for the way the old four-poster bed dominated the space.

"You sure that thing isn't a twin?" she asked.

"Having second thoughts? I can see if they have another room available."

She lifted her face to meet his gaze. Tired, battered and more than a little the worse for wear, she still exuded an attraction that surprised him every time.

"You're a nice man, R.J."

"At least you didn't call me sweet."

She smiled tiredly. "Do I look totally stupid?"

"No, you look beautiful."

He hadn't meant to say that. Her eyes widened in surprise. A glint of excitement stirred in their depths.

"But battered," he hastily added. He turned away and flicked on the other bedside lamp. "Will you be okay to get ready for bed on your own? I want to run down to the bar for a minute. I spotted a guy in there I need to talk with."

He was pretty sure she knew he was lying, but she squeezed his arm as she passed him heading for the bathroom. "Take your time, R.J. I'll be fine."

Feeling unaccountably awkward, he pocketed the key card and left the room. To his surprise, he found both Kathy and Mrs. Norwhich sitting at a corner table munching pretzels. Fancy glasses with umbrellas sat in front of them, and an empty beer bottle and glass sat next to Kathy at an empty seat. Kathy motioned him over. After ordering a beer, he joined them, taking the fourth chair.

"Will went to the men's room," Kathy explained. "How's Teri?"

"A mild concussion and some bruises. She didn't even need stitches."

"Good. I was worried about her."

"May I ask you something? Is Heartskeep haunted?"

Startled by the abrupt question, Kathy shook her head. "No," she replied quickly. R.J. had the impression she was rattled.

"'Course it is," Mrs. Norwhich scoffed.

"I've never seen a ghost," Kathy insisted.

Mrs. Norwhich snorted. "Never seen her, either, but I've felt her many a time. Icy cold, she is. I even heard her crying once when I used the hidden stairs to put some towels in one of the bedrooms."

"Which hidden stairs?" R.J. interrupted.

"The ones off the spare room downstairs. Some fool went and boarded them up, but they save me a heap of walking."

Another mystery solved.

"The ghost is a her?" R.J. asked.

"That's my impression and you can stop looking at me like I'm some crazy old woman, Kathy Walsh. I know you know about her. You lived there lots longer than me. But I've lived years longer than you. Long enough to know there's plenty of things in this world no one can explain."

"Leigh and I saw her once when we were little kids," Kathy said quietly after a few minutes.

R.J. tried not to gape.

"Well, we saw something." She shrugged self-consciously. "More of a white mist than a real shape if you see what I mean. I haven't thought about that in years."

Will joined them a few minutes later and the talk turned to a rehash of the evening's events. By the time R.J. finished the beer he hadn't wanted in the first place, he was fairly certain Teri would be in bed asleep. And he was positive that he was tired enough to sleep despite the distraction her presence was going to cause.

The others walked with him as far as the second floor. He continued on up to the third and let himself into the room as quietly as possible.

Teri was buried under the heavy down comforter, her eyes closed. She'd left the light glowing softly on his side of the bed, and R.J. used the bathroom as quietly as possible.

A real gentleman would have slept in his jeans, but R.J.'s were too dirty and stained. Since he only had one other pair with him, he decided Teri was mature enough not to freak if he slept in his briefs. He crossed the room to the bed and shut off the lamp, slipping under the warm covers.

"R.J.?"

"Go back to sleep."

She cuddled closer, raising his blood pressure along with his libido.

"Learn anything?" Teri whispered.

"Yeah. Mrs. Norwhich likes piña coladas, Kathy likes mai tais, Will likes beer and Heartskeep is definitely haunted by a cold white mist."

"Thought so. Can we go to sleep now?"

"I sure as heck hope so."

He closed his eyes, filled with doubt.

When he opened them again, sunlight was filtering in past the drapes and Teri was staring into his eyes from the pillow beside him. R.J. realized his arm was around her, pinning her in place.

"'Morning," she said softly.

He felt his erection pressing against the softness of her thigh where their legs were entwined. Teri didn't seem alarmed, so he relaxed.

Cupping her face lightly he studied the bruise skirting the side of her face. Tenderly, he touched the battered skin with a butterfly caress.

"How's your head?"

"Coma-free."

"No thanks to me. I didn't do such a good job checking on you last night, did I?"

"You kept me warm," she grinned.

"Glad to know I'm good for something."

"Oh, I imagine you're good for a few other things, as well."

Blood sang in his veins. "Yeah?"

His mouth hovered inches from hers. His body filled with a sensual longing. The same trembling excitement was reflected in her expression. She was warm and soft, and he felt her need as an extension of his own.

"I should get up."

She met his gaze without blinking. "Is there some hurry?"

"You're injured," he reminded both of them.

The smile started in her eyes. "Not where it counts."

"But your head—"

"Isn't going to fall off if you make love to me."

Relieved that he hadn't imagined her desire, he smiled slowly. "Good to know."

R.J. drew her face to his gently. As his lips settled over hers, she kissed him back with a burning greed that set his body ablaze. He quickly discovered Teri was wearing nothing more than a thin, oversize T-shirt.

"No wonder you were cold."

"It's more than I normally wear."

R.J. smiled. "Then let's get rid of it."

He stripped off his briefs, then slid the edges of her shirt up and over the flatness of her belly and the firm round curve of her pink-tipped breasts. Gently, he tugged it over her scalp until there was nothing between them but skin and the slick, wet heat of eager passion.

With mouth and tongue and lips and hands, he played her body until the crescendo of excitement built beyond tolerance. She climaxed in his hand, crying his name. Instead of taking his own pleasure, he waited, kissing her gently, stroking her softly, and loving her as if she were something infinitely precious, until her pleasure became a wanting once more and the wanting became unbearable. Only then did he fit himself above her and ease inside, spurred on by the frantic sound of her pleasure as he drove them toward the release they both craved.

"I love you," she murmured helplessly against his throat as she climaxed. Utterly spent, she fell back asleep in his arms, the scent of their lovemaking filling the air.

TERI AWOKE TO THE SOUND of a housekeeping cart being wheeled down the hall outside her door. Even before she opened her eyes she knew R.J. was gone. Swearing, she sat up and peered around.

The earlier sunlight had been replaced by a dismal gray light that settled heavily over the room. It didn't sound as if it was raining, but it might as well have been. And it was nearly nine-thirty.

Her head hurt, and her body ached in places that had nothing to do with yesterday and everything to do with what had happened this morning. The taste and scent of R.J. filled her.

And she wanted him again, right now.

Teri winced. Had she really told him she loved him? No wonder he was gone. In his position, she would have run as well.

Moving stiffly, she found her nightshirt neatly folded on the dresser. Great. He was not only a considerate lover, he was a tidy one.

A shower did little to improve her mood. Her breasts were sensitive and her thighs were sore. Whisker burns had turned her skin red in several sensitive places. Teri alternated between embarrassment at her wild abandon and anger for being so stupid as to want their lovemaking to mean more than a simple tumble.

How could she have told him she loved him?

The strong physical attraction had been there from the first, but that was all it could be. It made sense. After all, R.J. was everything a woman could want in a man or a lover. Teri would not waste one minute regretting what they'd done.

But she couldn't stop reliving it as she showered and dressed. It struck her as she was putting on her shoes that if The Inn was local place to stay, Lester might very well have taken a room here.

Fear nestled in her belly, spreading tentacles all through her. Why hadn't she thought of that last night?

He could be here, right down the hall. Heck, he could be in the room next door!

She was fine, she told herself. It had been Russell, not Lester, who had invaded Heartskeep. Lester hadn't recognized her yesterday. He probably hadn't even noticed her aunt's car.

But what if he had?

It didn't matter. He had no way of knowing she was here. But her fear gathered momentum. She didn't have her gun any longer and she was sitting around a hotel room like a mouse in a trap.

She had to get out of here!

Except that her car was at Heartskeep several miles away. She had her wallet, money and a credit card, but she didn't have Corey. If Lester wasn't here, he would be doing all he could to find his son.

Lester would also know Corey was her goal if he had recognized her.

Would a town this small have a car rental place? She'd settle for a cab to take her out to Heartskeep.

The sudden tap on her door stopped her in midpace. She swung around, heart pounding. Lester wouldn't knock, she reasoned.

A key was inserted into the lock. Teri felt a wave of relief as R.J. stepped inside, holding a tray with two cups of steaming coffee and an assortment of pastries.

Her heart gave a lurch at the sight of him. The perfectly fitted jeans, green sweater and light blue shirt he wore beneath an open navy windbreaker could have been tailor-made for him.

He set down the tray on the small writing desk. At the last second, something kept her from flinging herself into his arms. He wasn't smiling. The strain of the past twenty-four hours showed clearly on his face. Something was very wrong.

He handed her a foam cup of coffee. "Eastman came through surgery. He's expected to live, but a bullet lodged against his spine. It looks as though he'll be paralyzed from the waist down."

"At least Evelyn and Ian won't have to worry about him coming after them again."

"No."

Teri hated the stiff awkwardness that had fallen between them. She knew every inch of his body, yet he seemed a dark, forbidding stranger this morning.

"I brought you some Danish."

"I'm not hungry." Not anymore.

Where was the gentle lover from last night? R.J. was more than distant, he was angry beneath that polite facade.

She set the coffee down untasted. "What's wrong?"

"I spoke to Wyatt a few minutes ago. Boyington's marriage to Valerie wasn't legal," he told her with a closed expression. "His marriage to Rosalynn wasn't legal, either."

Her heart fluttered. "What do you mean?"

"According to the information Wyatt has now, Boyington married a girl two years before Rosalynn. They were living in a rental condo in Florida. Then one day they weren't. He'd paid through the end of the month, but they moved out in the middle of the night without leaving a forwarding address. There's no record of a divorce or a death certificate anywhere. For all intents and purposes, the first Mrs. Boyington simply disappeared."

A numbing fear oozed through her insides. "And I'll bet she didn't have any family, did she?"

"No. She was an orphan."

Teri couldn't prevent a shudder. "He prefers them that way."

"You seem to know a lot about him."

She didn't reply. His blue eyes darkened.

"Rosalynn had an older sister."

She knew what came next. "You know, don't you?"

"Why don't you tell me."

"I'm not a private investigator."

"Your name isn't Teri, either," he stated without a flicker in his inflection or his stare.

"Actually, Theresa is my middle name. Lorraine Theresa Johnson."

"You're a freelance nature photographer."

"Yes."

"You've been in Africa for more than a year working on a documentary."

"Yes. Because I travel so much, I guess Rosalynn seemed like an orphan to Lester since our parents are dead."

Mutely, Teri waited, unable to say all the things bottled up inside her. Why hadn't she told him everything sooner?

"You returned to the States a few months ago and flew to Texas to see your sister."

Each word was a nail of condemnation. Teri was helpless to stop the flow and unable to muster a defense.

"And found her living a nightmare," she agreed.

"Your aunt is an ophthalmologist," he continued. "Her husband is a well-respected plastic surgeon. They live fairly close to where Rosalynn and Boyington rented their house."

"We weren't close to our extended family."

"I didn't notice any camera equipment in your bag."

He'd gone through her bag?

"You came here to get Corey, didn't you?"

"Of course I did! Everything I've done has been for Corey."

His jaw hardened. "Well, you don't have to worry. The police won't turn him over to Boyington now. Not until they investigate all this. Why didn't you go through legal channels to get him?"

"You don't understand!"

"So make me understand."

She hated his anger, knowing he felt betrayed by her silence.

"Rosalyn is in a coma in a private hospital in Texas. She's registered under an alias. The doctors don't know if she'll ever wake up. If she does, they don't know how much of her will be left. Lester did that to her. If he learns we're alive, he'll do everything in his power to kill us."

"The police—"

"Play by the rules. Don't you get it? Lester doesn't. He's a contract killer, R.J.!"

"We still don't know that for certain."

"How many bodies does it take?"

His jaw hardened. "Why didn't you tell me who you were before?"

"I couldn't afford to trust anyone. All I wanted was to find Corey and get him as far from Lester as I could."

"You trusted me last night. Enough to make love to me. You could have told me the truth then."

"Is that what this is all about? Your ego? Yes, I made love with you. So what?"

His expression grew even harsher. "You tell all your partners you love them?"

No, she wanted to shout, but his closed expression made that impossible. "Don't tell me you've never said that to one of your conquests at the height of excitement."

"I haven't," he said with cold finality.

And he hadn't said it to her, either.

A timid knock on the door sent both their heads swiveling in that direction. R.J. motioned her to silence as he crossed to the peephole and peered out. Swearing softly, he reached for the handle, flinging open the door.

"Valerie?"

Stunned, Teri stared as R.J. stepped forward and hugged the frail-looking woman standing there. Dressed in jeans and a jacket that hung badly on a too thin frame, she'd added a work hat and dark glasses that effectively covered most of her battered features. Behind her, another young woman was dressed in a similar, if better-fitting, style, minus the hat and glasses. Worry nibbled at her expression.

"May we come in?" Valerie asked nervously.

"Of course." R.J. ushered them inside. "I know you," he said to the second woman. "Carla Boggs, right? You and your dad work for the Walkens."

"Yes."

"Who are you?" Valerie demanded, coming to a stop when she saw Teri.

"Teri Johnson," she replied gently. "I'm very glad to see you're alive."

"Why?"

"Believe it or not, I came here to rescue you."

"And Corey," R.J. put in pointedly.

"Especially Corey," she agreed without looking at him.

"Teri is Corey's aunt," he added grimly.

"Oh, good. Then you already know he isn't mine. That's one of the things I came here to tell you. Lester told me he didn't have any other family or I would have brought him to you."

"Why did you run away like that, Valerie?"

Her eyes clouded. "Lester didn't give me a choice. I thought I'd be safe at Heartskeep, but he found me right away."

"He saw the e-mails," Teri explained.

"But I deleted them!"

"He was probably able to recover them off your hard drive," Teri suggested.

"What happened the other night?" R.J. asked.

"Lester called my cell phone after I went upstairs. The phone is brand-new so I don't know how he got the number, but he said he was outside by the fountain. If I didn't come out he'd come in and start killing people. He would have, R.J.! He killed Todd just for trying to fix my car for me!"

"Todd would be the man whose parents lived next door to you?" Teri asked.

"Yes. He was such a nice guy. I mean, really nice. We got to talking down by the mailbox one day. I was so unhappy with Lester gone all the time and trapped out there by myself with just the baby. Even though he is a doll and so well behaved," she added quickly. "I was starved for adult companionship. I told Todd how the car wouldn't run and Lester said we couldn't afford to get it fixed. Todd said he was good with cars. He had time to have a look if I liked."

She closed her eyes, her face was such a picture of despair Teri's heart wrenched.

"I knew Lester was due back that day, but he didn't

usually come home until late. He showed up when Todd was lifting the hood for a look. I could tell he was really mad. Oh, he was nice to Todd, but his eyes were so cold. I was scared. I didn't know what to do. Lester told Todd he'd already hired someone from town to come out and look at the car."

She began to pace restlessly. "I knew he was lying. I could tell. But what could I say? Then he invited Todd to stay for dinner. There was an intensity about him that terrified me. Todd didn't even seem to realize the danger. There was nothing I could do."

Teri felt her helplessness as clearly as if it had been her own.

"Todd liked him, I could tell. And Lester couldn't have been more charming. Only, when Todd wasn't looking Lester would turn this dark look on me that made me want to throw up. I knew he was furious, but I never in a million years thought he'd kill Todd."

"But he did?" R.J. demanded.

"I can't prove it. I don't even know where he buried the body. But I know he killed him. He kept Todd's wineglass full all through dinner. Todd wasn't sloppy drunk or anything, but he shouldn't have gotten behind the wheel, despite the coffee Lester made him drink afterward. I felt sick. I didn't know what to do. Finally Todd left and Lester just stood there looking at me. I was so darn scared."

Teri started to reach for her, but Carla slid a comforting arm around her friend. "It wasn't your fault, Val. You know it wasn't."

"I should have done something. I should have warned him. But I'd never seen Lester like that."

"He'd never hit you before?" Teri asked.

"No way," she said firmly. "I would never have stayed

with him if he'd hit me. Although he'd done other things..." She turned away, embarrassed.

"He eroded your self-confidence," Teri said knowingly. "You could never please him. Every compliment came with a dig. He'd point out your blouse was pretty but it showed you were gaining a little weight, or the house looked good except for the bathroom floor."

Teri was aware of R.J.'s sharp gaze on her.

"Exactly! He was always going on about my weight. I was starving myself trying to please him because he could be so sweet. I know that sounds crazy, but—"

"No, it's part of his pattern," Teri told her. "He beats you down mentally until you'll offer no resistance, because who'd believe you, anyhow? He's such a charming, handsome, likable man."

She clamped her jaw tightly on the suppressed fury building inside her.

"That's it exactly. Only everything changed that night. He told me to put the baby to bed and wait for him upstairs. He said he had a quick errand to run and he'd be right back. I knew something was horribly wrong. I mean, where would he go at that hour of the night? Fools Point goes Cinderella at the stroke of ten. There wasn't anything open."

Teri nodded in understanding while Carla squeezed Valerie's arm. A muscle twitched in R.J.'s face, the only sign of the control he was exerting.

"I probably would have taken Corey and left right then if I'd had a car, but I kept telling myself everything would be okay. I tried to convince myself I was overreacting, even though I knew I wasn't. And then he didn't come back for hours."

She was shaking. So was Teri. It was as if she were living the nightmare with Valerie.

"I wanted to believe he was driving around to cool off. I kept thinking he was jealous and I should be flattered, but I wasn't. I wanted him to be fine when he got home so I could explain, but I was afraid. I pretended I was asleep when he finally did come back. He knew I wasn't, but he didn't say anything at first. He was whistling as got ready for bed. Whistling! He even took a shower. Only he always showered in the morning. I'm sure he was washing away the evidence from killing Todd."

She stopped on a sob.

"He beat and raped you, didn't he?" Teri asked softly.

She nodded, not looking at them. "He...he said I belonged to him. And he said I wouldn't have to worry about Todd coming around to bother me again. Nothing I said seemed to matter to him. It was as if I wasn't even human any more."

"No, your words wouldn't have mattered. You weren't human to him, just another possession. One he wanted to punish."

Teri felt R.J.'s eyes boring into her but she didn't care. There was no way to put things right with him at this point.

Valerie nodded through her tears. "He got off on hurting me. It was as though that's what he'd been waiting for."

"It was," Teri agreed. "He likes to hurt women. It makes him feel powerful."

"Yes. That's it exactly." Valerie wiped at her eyes angrily. "I knew I had to get away, but I couldn't leave Corey there with a monster. I had to pretend to be cowed until I could figure out where to go and how."

"That's when you found me on the Internet?" R.J. asked.

Valerie nodded. "He always kept the door to his office locked, but I knew how to get it open. The computer was my only link to friends, you see. I was always careful not to disturb anything.

"The day I left, I searched his office. There was nothing there, but in the breast pocket of the suit he'd worn the day before I found a list of names. Two had been crossed off. I realized both names had been in the news recently."

"We found the list, Valerie," Teri told her.

"Why didn't you go to the police with it?" R.J. questioned.

"I didn't trust them. Lester talked about the police chief like they were friends. I was terrified."

She stared at them starkly. "He'd been killing people and coming home to me. It was a nightmare! A sick nightmare. I hid the list in Corey's toy dog. I'd seen it done in a movie once. I planned to send it to the state police anonymously after I got to Heartskeep, but I never got the chance."

Carla hugged her in sympathy. "It's okay. No one is blaming you."

"I know, but…" Her thin shoulders rose and fell helplessly. "I blame me. Look how many more names on that list have died because I was too afraid to do the right thing. I knew the marriage was a mistake almost from the start, but I was so lonely after my dad died. And Lester can be so charming."

"His stock in trade," Teri agreed.

"But how did he get my new cell phone number?" she asked.

Teri shrugged. "Your new provider may have called the house to check on your service, or they sent you a bill."

"The question is how he got on the grounds to Heartskeep that night," R.J. muttered.

"There's a back gate past the old barns," Valerie told him. "It was open when I left."

"Jacob," R.J. said darkly with a quick glance at Teri. "How did you get away from Boyington?"

"She stabbed the bastard," Carla said with relish. "Show them! He for sure wasn't expecting her to meet him armed. Too bad she didn't kill him."

Valerie ignored her friend and pulled a large kitchen knife from inside her coat.

"Mrs. Norwhich mentioned a missing kitchen knife," R.J. exclaimed. "I remember being worried at the time. I thought maybe Ian had taken it to use on his patrols, but I forgot to ask him."

"I took it when I went out to meet him," Valerie admitted. "When he grabbed me, I stabbed him as hard as I could. Then I ran. He was so surprised. I hoped he'd die. And if that makes me a horrible person, I don't care."

"The only horrible person is Lester," Teri told her firmly. "And you *did* hurt him. Remember how stiffly he carried himself, R.J.? He said he'd been in a car accident."

"I keep hoping it'll turn septic and he'll die a slow, painful death," Valerie added viciously.

"I told Val to go to the police," Carla said, "but she said they couldn't protect her."

"They can't," both women said together.

"How did you get involved?" R.J. asked Carla.

"I'd stayed late to keep an eye on a colicky horse. Dad and I work in the stables," she added for Teri's benefit. "I nearly hit Val with my car when she darted across the road. I knew her from when she used to live here, but I barely recognized her. I wanted to call Wyatt right away, but she begged me not to."

"I knew Kathy and Alexis would take care of Corey and I couldn't go back. I won't be safe until I can dance on his grave."

"She's right," Teri agreed.

R.J. ignored that. "How did you know to come here this morning?"

"We didn't. The power's out at Carla's house, so we drove over to get breakfast."

"I saw you getting coffee at the breakfast bar," Carla added, "and followed you up here. Only I wasn't sure exactly which room you went into, so we took a chance."

"I wanted you to know about Corey, R.J. And to tell you about the list of names. We need to get going now."

"Where?"

"Someplace where Lester will never find me."

R.J. shook his head. "Stay and talk to the police, Valerie. They're going to take him down."

"I don't think so," Valerie disagreed. "Lester believes he's invincible. I'm not so sure he isn't. He'll concoct a story. It's what he's good at."

"It won't do him any good. You and Teri can testify against him. And then there's that list of names."

Valerie shook her head, fear in her eyes.

"That list of names condemns," Teri interjected, "but it isn't proof of anything, R.J. All it will take is a good attorney to muddy that list. When was it written? How many of us handled it? Are his fingerprints even still on it? How many handwriting experts will swear it isn't his handwriting?"

She tried to keep her anger and frustration from

spilling over. "Circumstantial evidence won't convict Lester. That's why I haven't come forward to charge him with assault and attempted murder. It's my word against his. He can be so convincing. You don't know him!"

"She's right," Valerie agreed. "The laws protect the guilty as often as the victims."

"Ask any woman who's ever applied for a restraining order," Teri added. "A piece of paper is not going to keep a man away from a woman he considers his possession. Would it stop *you* if you were determined?"

R.J. looked grim. Carla appeared frightened.

"So you're going to run again, Valerie?"

"Yes. And if you two were smart, you'd do the same thing. I'm sorry I got you involved in this, R.J., but thanks for trying to help me."

"And thank you for taking such good care of Corey," Teri said with heartfelt gratitude.

For the first time, Valerie smiled. "He's a loveable little guy. I hope his mom pulls through. I really do."

Her heart lurched, but Valerie was already heading for the door.

"Goodbye, R.J. Come on, Carla."

Teri gave R.J. credit for watching them leave without trying to stop them.

"She's right, you know," Teri told him as soon as he closed the door. "We should go, too. Lester may have taken a room here as well."

"No. I checked that before I brought you here. He must have gone to one of the places out on the highway."

She knew she should feel relieved, but she didn't. "Stony Ridge is a small place, R.J. If they can find us, so can he."

"All right. I'll take you to George and Emily's place. The Walkens were my foster parents."

"No. You don't want to put anyone else at risk."

"Corey's there."

Chapter Fourteen

"Let's go!"

R.J.'s expression shut down completely. He walked to the door and held it open. He said nothing, waiting for her to precede him into the hall. She wanted to tell him that she did trust him. That, unbelievably, her words of love hadn't been empty. But she couldn't say it. As soon as she had Corey, she'd be gone. Her nephew had to come first.

"I wanted to tell you everything, but trust will never come easily to me again," she told him.

"I take it you tried to help your sister escape?"

"Yes. If she dies, it will be my fault."

"How do you figure that?"

"I should have planned things better."

"What happened?"

"Pretty much a replica of what happened to Valerie. Lester found out she was planning to leave and came home early. He beat her unconscious, then he waited for me."

She shuddered, unwilling to remember what had happened then.

"After I was unconscious, he put us in her car and drove us to where the flooding was at its worst. He must have had it planned in advance because he had another car there waiting. He put our car in gear and sent it into the water."

R.J. muttered something under his breath.

"I came to when the car was filling with water. Rosalynn was trying to get us out through the window. I'm not sure exactly how it happened, but suddenly we were in the open water being slammed by debris. We're both strong swimmers but no one could swim in that. I knew we were going to die."

R.J. stopped walking, but Teri thought it was easier to tell him while they kept moving so she strode ahead of him through the lobby, lost in the nightmare.

"The current pushed her into a tree. Somehow, incredibly, she managed to grab my arm. She helped me onto a thick branch and tried to climb up with me. Something smashed her against the trunk. I barely managed to hold her there. She was unconscious, badly hurt…."

Teri shuddered. It was yesterday in her mind. She could hear the roar of the water, feel its pull as unseen objects battered them. She swallowed hard.

"Everything gets a little vague after that. I remember some people coming to our rescue, but not exactly how they got us free. Rosalynn has been in a coma ever since."

Outside, the sky was depressingly overcast, a vivid reminder of that other dark stretch of days. While it wasn't raining, the threat hung there as dark as her memories. Despite her churning stomach, Teri was doing her best to distance her emotions from the words she'd recited.

In silence, R.J. led her to her aunt's small car rather than his battered truck.

"I thought you would find it easier to get in and out of the car."

"How did you get it here?"

"Wyatt had one of his men drop it off for me." He held out the key. "Do you want to drive?"

"No. You know where we're going."

Holding the car door open, he met her gaze. "I know it's worthless, but I'm sorry for what you went through, Teri."

Unable to speak past the lump in her throat, she nodded and slid into the car, staring straight ahead. Pity was the last thing she wanted from R.J.

He closed the door without saying more and strode around to get in beside her. Pulling on his seat belt, he started the engine.

The gun came over the back seat in a blur so fast there was no time to react. R.J.'s head jerked to one side as the muzzle was pressed against his skull. Teri couldn't breathe. Lester's expression was furious.

"Get us out of here, hero. I *will* kill you if you don't. Then I'll kill her and take the car."

Panic riveted her to the seat.

"You'll kill us anyway," R.J. said flatly.

"True. But you can buy yourself a few more minutes to live if you drive. And while you're doing it, you can sit there and plan how you think you'll escape. But if you move another inch, Lori, he's dead. Now drive!"

Teri froze the hand that had been unconsciously reaching toward the gun. R.J. put the car in gear and pulled out of the parking lot.

"Where's your sister?"

"Dead."

"I don't think so, more's the pity. But she will be. You're going to take me to her."

The coldness spread, taking her past the realm of fear. "In your dreams, Lester. I'm not telling you anything."

His smile chilled her to the bone. "I love a challenge. I guess you need a refresher course."

He slammed the gun into the side of her face. R.J. deliberately wrenched the steering wheel hard left, despite the oncoming pickup truck in that lane. Lester was thrown to one side. The gun discharged harmlessly into the roof as the car plunged down the embankment under a canopy of trees.

Brush and branches tore at the metal as the vehicle bounced along out of control. Then the car hit a stone outcropping and went airborne for a heart-stopping moment.

Lester screamed as he was pitched forward between them. Teri was thrown against the seat belt as the car raced toward the rushing water below.

"TERI!"

She struggled to focus on R.J.'s face.

"Come on. We have to get out."

Her sluggish brain was slow to take in the situation. Water rushed over her feet, rising with fearsome speed. The windshield was badly cracked. The car bobbed and twisted in the rapidly moving current. R.J. had unfastened his seat belt. He was struggling to get hers undone, as well, but he moved awkwardly, his features creased in pain.

"You're hurt!"

"Shoulder's dislocated and I cracked a couple of ribs," R.J. told her. "Let's go!"

The water was nearly to her knees. Panic gripped her. She couldn't! It was happening all over again, and her terror was absolute.

"Snap out of it Teri! I can't do this alone."

The windows began to lower as he pressed a button. Nightmare memories superimposed themselves over the scene. Darkness. The smell of the rain and mud. The sound of the rushing water.

She sobbed out loud. It wasn't night. It wasn't raining. And R.J. needed help, or they would die.

He leaned between the seats, struggling with Lester's inert, bloody body. R.J. ripped the gun from his limp fingers and handed it to her. She stared at that blood-smeared, hated face. Lester opened glazed eyes. He looked straight at her without comprehension.

"Teri. No! You don't want to do that."

She hadn't consciously aimed the gun at his head, but with every fiber of her being she wanted to pull the trigger.

"That's his way, not yours."

R.J. covered her hand with his. She lowered the gun, and the car slammed to a jolting halt. R.J. gasped in pain as he was pitched against the steering column. She wrenched her back when she hit the dashboard. Lester also cried out as he smashed against the back of her seat.

Their vehicle had become lodged on something between a pair of trees. Water crested over the seat, still rising.

"Come on Boyington, you have to help." R.J. tried to force the man toward the open window.

Lester struggled free of his grip, his eyes wild.

People were slipping and sliding down the embankment toward them. The car shifted. Hands reached in through the window on her side of the car.

"Grab my hand."

"R.J.!" she protested.

"We'll get him next," the man promised. "Hurry before it shifts again."

Teri allowed his strong hands to pull her free. The car stirred once more as the current tugged at the hapless metal.

"Get R.J.!"

A second pair of hands grabbed her as her rescuer turned back to the car.

"Give me your hand," the man commanded. "Hurry!"

Teri plunged back toward the car to help as the two men fought to pull R.J. free. He slipped through the window and there came a grating sound. Abruptly, the car was sucked away. Teri screamed. She would have slipped into the grasping water if strong arms hadn't gripped her, yanking her back. R.J. was staggering onto the embankment.

She turned back toward the water in time to see the front of the car start to sink. Her gaze locked on Lester's terrified expression. A second later, the car sank from view.

They stood in silence, waiting, but Lester never bobbed to the surface and the water continued to rise.

"I'm sorry. We have to climb higher. There's nothing we can do," the man told her.

Teri looked him in the eye. "Good."

She turned back to R.J., whose face was wreathed in pain.

"Help's on the way," the older man was saying. "You're going to be okay."

She scrambled to R.J.'s side. "Don't you dare die on me! Do you hear me, R.J.? Don't you dare!"

"Deaf man...could hear you," he gasped weakly.

She touched her forehead to his and sobbed. "I love you," she whispered.

Ice-cold wet fingers squeezed hers. Then he shut his eyes.

"YOU'RE ONE LUCKY mother's son, you know that?" Wyatt said conversationally as he pulled out of the hospital parking lot hours later. "If that rib had punctured your lung…"

R.J. pressed back as Teri squeezed his fingers lightly. She'd stayed by his side, refusing treatment for her own cuts and scrapes until she was certain he was okay. Even then, he'd had to insist she let the doctor check her out.

R.J. was trying hard not to read too much into her actions, but he hadn't forgotten her whispered words as he struggled for breath past the pain in his chest. She hadn't been in the throes of passion then. Could it be she really meant it?

They barely knew one another. She hadn't trusted him. Yet that no longer seemed important. Part of him even understood. He'd known almost the minute he'd laid eyes on her that Teri was different from anyone he'd ever known. She had such courage and sheer determination. Maybe if she was willing to hang around, to give herself time to really get to know him—

Only she wouldn't hang around, would she? She was a wildlife photographer who traveled all over the world. He almost wished she was the private investigator she'd pretended to be.

Wyatt's cell phone rang. "Crossley…. They did? They got a positive ID? They're sure it's him?… Good," he met R.J.'s gaze. "I don't think anyone will be sorry to learn Lester Boyington is dead…. Yeah…. For who?… She's right here. Can you patch it through?"

He looked at Teri expectantly while he listened to someone speaking to him. "No, Doctor, this is Chief Crossley. One moment, your niece is right here."

"Olivia?" Teri asked incredulously.

"You need to take this call," he told her with a smile, handing her the telephone.

"Olivia, what…? She did…? She is?" Her eyes filled with tears. "Are they sure there's no damage?… Oh, thank God. Thank God!"

Tears filled her eyes.

"Yes….No. Lester is dead…. Yes, I'm sure." She looked at Wyatt, and he nodded. "He drowned. They pulled his body from the river…. I know. Poetic justice. It's a long story. I'll call you later with the details…. Yes, I'm fine. I'm on my way to Corey right now…. I know. Give Rosalynn my love. Tell her I'll see her soon."

Tears ran freely down her face as she turned to R.J. "My sister woke up an hour ago. There doesn't seem to be any permanent damage. The doctors think she's going to make a full recovery."

He held her awkwardly as she buried her face against his uninjured shoulder and cried softly for a few minutes. R.J. and Wyatt shared a look in the rearview mirror.

"Thanks for coming out and driving us all the way out here, Wyatt."

"I'm just glad the two of you are all right. Looks like you have a waiting committee."

Lights gleamed a steady welcome from the Walken windows as they pulled in front of the spacious house that had been R.J.'s home for so many years.

"I'm a mess," Teri muttered, trying to smooth her hair and straightened her mud-caked clothing.

"So am I. They won't care," he assured her.

Wyatt stopped the car but made no move to get out.

"Aren't you coming in?"

"Nope. I'm going home to *my* family. You two can handle yours without my help. We'll talk tomorrow."

"Thanks again, Wy."

"Yes, thank you," Teri added.

The front door of the house opened. Lucky bolted out to meet them.

"Hey, boy. How ya doin'? Did you think I forgot about you?"

The large dog greeted them effusively, his stubby tail wagged for all it was worth. And a little boy ran onto the porch calling after him.

Fresh tears blurred her eyes. Teri floated forward and dropped down to his level. "Hi, Corey. You probably don't even remember me, do you?"

"Doggy!"

"Lucky," she agreed. The large dog came over to swipe her face with his sandpaper tongue. For good measure, he licked Corey, nearly sending the boy sprawling. Corey laughed infectiously.

"Let's get inside before the doggy knocks you over. I don't about you, but I've rolled in enough mud for one day," R.J. said.

"Dirty," Corey agreed.

"Very dirty."

EMILY AND GEORGE WALKEN sat on the sofa, letting their coffee cool as they watched the bruised pair trying to help Corey build a tower out of wood blocks. Every few minutes, Lucky would come along and knock it down again. Corey would laugh uproariously, and they would mock-scold the dog and set about rebuilding.

"Do you think it's too early to start planning the wedding?" Emily asked her husband.

George smiled fondly. "They have a few issues to work through first but based on the glances they keep sending each other, I'd say you can start thinking about it."

"Even Lucky and Corey approve," she told him happily.

George lifted her hand and placed a kiss on the lightly wrinkled skin. She smiled back at him and he settled more firmly in his seat, content to know that another of their problem children had found the perfect partner.

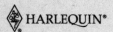

If you enjoyed what you just read,
then we've got an offer you can't resist!

Take 2 bestselling love stories FREE!

Plus get a FREE surprise gift!